I wanted her to be some evil demon who'd stolen my husband with promises of chandelier sex and perfect baked Alaska.

But as I looked into her blue eyes—such a vibrant color compared to my own plain brown ones—I couldn't hate her.

"I didn't know," she said, taking a step closer, lowering her voice. "Not until I read the obituary in the paper."

I decided to believe her. If he'd fooled me for fifteen years, surely he could have fooled her, too. A hundred questions filled my mind, but before I could speak his mother was reaching for me. So I gave the other wife a slight, dismissive nod, and slipped back into the perfect portrait of what everyone expected of me.

Out of the corner of my eye I saw her walk away. We were members of the same club now, she and I.

I hoped like hell I wasn't going to find anyone else with a membership before this day was over.

Shirley Jump

Bookseller's Best Award winner Shirley Jump didn't have the willpower to diet or the talent to master under-eye concealer, so she bowed out of a career in television and opted instead for a career where she could be paid to eat at her desk—writing. In the worlds Shirley gets to create and control, the children listen to their parents, the husbands always remember holidays and the housework is magically done by elves.

She sold her first book to Silhouette Books in 2001 and now writes stories about love, family and food—the three most important things in her life (order reversible, depending on the day)—using that English degree everyone said would be useless.

Though she's thrilled to see her books in stores around the world, Shirley mostly writes because it gives her an excuse to avoid housework and helps feed her shoe habit.

To read excerpts or just find information on her latest title, visit her Web site at www.shirleyjump.com.

THE OTHER WIFE

SHIRLEY JUMP

THE OTHER WIFE

Copyright © 2006 by Shirley Kawa-Jump

isbn-13:978-0-373-88118-5

isbn-10:   0-373-88118-5

This edition published by arrangement with Harlequin Books S.A.

® and TM are trademarks of the publisher. Trademarks indicated with
® are registered in the United States Patent and Trademark Office, the
Canadian Trade Marks Office and in other countries.

TheNextNovel.com

 HARLEQUIN®

PRINTED IN U.S.A.

From the Author

Dear Reader,

People always ask me if my stories are based on my real life. I can honestly say the bigamy part of this one is not, although the quest for change, for finding your place in the world, is a part of all of us. We grow up, but we may never grow away from things that hold us in place. Penny's quest is one that resonates with me, and I hope it does with you, too.

I don't own a Jack Russell terrier, and neither of my dogs can do anything more incredible than fetch the newspaper on snowy mornings, which isn't such a bad trick when it's hovering around zero. Max, Annie's dog, is based on my real-life Max, who forgets he's way too big to be a lapdog and is as incorrigible as a toddler.

I have loved reading the Harlequin NEXT line since it debuted and am thrilled and honored to be a part of it. This book was definitely a blast to write, and I hope you enjoy reading it as much as I enjoyed dreaming up the story line.

Shirley

To my good friend Janet Dean, who has helped me make every book better and supported me even when I thought there was no way I could pull off a funny story about a two-timing husband and his piano-playing dog.

Also, a big thanks to Joe Murphy and his adorable wonder dog, Katie, who has brought smiles to hundreds of people over the years.

Finally, as the owner of a shelter dog myself, a huge thank-you to all the hard workers and valuable volunteers at animal shelters across the country. Consider opening your heart and home to a rescue animal. Yours might not sing "The Star-Spangled Banner," but will undoubtedly bring some wondrous fun to your life.

CHAPTER I

The last person I expected to see at my husband's wake was his wife.

Yet, there she stood, to the right of his casket, wiping away her tears with a lacy white handkerchief, a fancy one with a tatted edge and an embroidered monogram, the kind your grandmother hands down to you because tissues aren't as ladylike.

She was tall, this other wife, probably five foot eight, and wearing strappy black heels with little rhinestones marching across the toe. I wanted to grab her, shake her and tell her those stupid shoes were completely inappropriate for the funeral of the man I'd been married to for fifteen years. *Go get yourself some pumps*, I wanted to scream. *Low-heeled, sensible, boring shoes*.

I wasn't mad at *her*. Exactly. I was madder than hell at the man lying on the top-grade satin in an elaborate, six-thousand-dollar cherry box, a peaceful expression on his cheating face.

Even in death, he looked ordinary and normal, the kind of guy you'd see on the street and think, oh, he's got the American Dream in his hands. A slight paunch over his belly from too many years behind his desk, the bald spot he'd been trying to hide with creative combing, the wrinkles around his eyes from finding humor in everything from the newspaper to the cereal box.

Just your typical forty-year-old man—a forty-year-old whom I had loved and thought would be sitting beside me on the porch, complaining about the neighbors' landscaping habits and debating a move to Florida, long into our old age. A man who could make me laugh on a dime, who'd thought nothing of surprising me with flowers, just because. He'd been a typical man in a hundred different ways—and so had our marriage.

Sure, a little dull at times, marked by trips to the dry cleaner on Tuesday and scrambled eggs every Sunday morning. But it had been a marriage, a partnership.

Or not, considering the two-wives-at-one-time thing, something I'd discovered last night in a picture of his double wedded bliss, stuffed behind the AmEx in his wallet.

Forty-eight hours ago, my life had been normal. While I was picking out a roast for dinner that night, paramedics had been rushing him into the hospital. Someone found my number on his cell phone because I, being the practical one, had seen some commercial about setting up an I.C.E. list, in case of emergency, and inputted my cell number. Dave, the spontaneous one, had laughed at me, but kept the number there.

The voice on the other end told me he'd had a heart attack. I'd rushed to Mass General, then stayed by his bedside fretting, pacing, shouting at the doctors to *do something*. But there wasn't anything they could do.

The Big Macs and Dave's habit of burning the candle on all ends had caught up with him.

Either that or the weight of his conscience had squished an aortic valve. In my less-charitable moments, I wanted to think it was the latter.

"Penny," someone said, laying a hand on my arm.

Kim Grant, my next-door neighbor, who had baked cupcakes to welcome Dave and me to the neighborhood last month, stood before me in the receiving line with a look of true sympathy on her face. A flash of guilt ran through me. I still hadn't returned her Tupperware container.

I hoped she wasn't in any rush for her plastic.

"Hi, Kim. Thanks for coming." The words flowed automatically, the same ones I'd said already a hundred times today, feeling sometimes that I was the one giving out comfort instead of receiving it.

Yet, even as I stood in Kim's embrace, in my peripheral vision, I was always aware of *her*, standing at the edge, blending in with the other mourners, as well as someone could blend when dressed like Marilyn Monroe. The insurance company my husband had worked for was large, and nearly a hundred people from the offices were there. I doubted anyone noticed her.

How many of them, I wondered, knew about her? Did anyone? Or did everyone?

Had I been the only one left out of the secret? The poor, silly wife, sitting at home with a pot roast waiting on the table, completely oblivious to the train wreck that had derailed her marriage.

I still didn't know her name, where she lived, or how long she'd been married to him. All I knew was that she'd been with my husband, in the Biblical sense, that day. Dave, the man who preferred T-shirts over sweatshirts and cotton blend over straight cotton, had been rushed into the E.R. *naked*. I knew he'd left the house dressed that day—I was the one who'd finished pressing his shirt while he hopped into the shower.

I thought of that shirt, remembering how I'd run my

hand over the flat fabric while it was still warm, pleased with the neat creases, then, later, the kiss Dave had given me as a thanks. The way he'd smelled of steam and starch and Stetson.

"That's the way we found him in the Marriott, ma'am," one of the paramedics told me, shrugging, as if it were completely ordinary to bring in a naked guy on a gurney.

"The Marriott?" I'd asked—twice—trying to get my head around that. Had it been a meeting gone wrong? A robbery? And then, the worst had hit me. "Was he—" I paused, my entire marriage flashing before my eyes like a jerky home movie, with edits I couldn't see, moments left on the cutting-room floor "—with anyone?"

"The, ah, bellhop said he checked in with his wife." The paramedic had looked at me hopefully. I didn't answer, letting the silence push him to add more. "She wasn't there, though. Apparently already left because they were, ah, done."

Done. I didn't have to ask what Dave had done. The nudity was a pretty good clue.

"I'm so sorry, Penny." Kim's voice drew me back to the present. "Dave was such a great guy."

I used to think that. Had even bragged about him

to my friends when we met, about how I got the last great guy on earth.

Apparently I wasn't the only one.

She crossed my line of vision again, as she read the tags on the flowers to the right of the casket. I maintained my position in the receiving line, stoic and reserved, the portrait of the grieving widow.

Lillian, Dave's mother, stood beside me, tears flowing nonstop, shoulders shaking a little as she cried. Still, Lillian Reynolds maintained a level of reserve, as always the gracious former debutante who'd married a lawyer. She didn't know about the second wife and I wasn't going to announce it between "ashes to ashes" and "dust to dust."

Maybe, I thought, if I never spoke the words, I could pretend it had never happened, that this other wife was a figment of my imagination.

"It was so sudden," Kim said, shaking her head as she looked at Dave.

As Kim continued speaking words I didn't hear, I glanced at my husband, lying there in his good blue suit, the one with the silver pinstripe that we'd picked out at JCPenney last Christmas, and for a second, felt a pang of grief so sharp I wanted to collapse. He was gone. Forever. For five seconds, I didn't care about the bigamy, didn't care what else he had hidden from me, I just wanted my husband back.

I wanted my life back, damn it. Rewind the clock, stop the tape, just get me out of this lily-scented twilight zone.

I wanted to be able to wake up, knowing that today would be the same as yesterday, that the numbered boxes on the wall calendar in the kitchen would follow one another with the reliable sameness of ironed shirts and scrambled eggs.

Insanely, I stared at his chest, willing it to rise and fall. It didn't.

So I stood there in Perkins & Sons Funeral Home, wearing a black suit I'd had to borrow from my sister because I was in no condition to shop, and trying not to picture my husband having a heart attack while he was on top of another woman, probably using the same well-practiced missionary moves he'd used on me last Saturday.

The Marriott, I'd found out, after pumping the paramedic a little more, was in downtown Newton. A convenient location. But for whom? For him? For her? The hotel was only three miles from our house. Close enough that he could have stopped by for a little afternoon delight with me. Also close enough that had

I gone to my usual Thursday manicure instead of going to a last-minute client meeting, I would have passed right by the hotel parking lot and maybe seen the "Insurance: The Investment for Those You Love" bumper sticker on his Benz.

For a guy who worked in risk management, he'd clearly liked to live on the edge.

I stepped back from the casket, from the cloying fragrance of the enormous white bouquet sent by the company, pressing a tissue to my eyes, willing my own tears to stop. I was mad at him, mad at myself, mad at the world. And yet, another part of me just wanted to curl up in the corner.

Kim finished whatever it was she had to say to me, so I smiled politely and thanked her for coming. She released me and moved to stand in front of Dave, dropping to the kneeler and making the sign of the cross over her chest.

I had a few uncharitable thoughts about God just then, ones that I was sure were going to get me sent to hell, so I turned away from my husband to do what needed to be done.

Face the other wife.

She skipped signing the guest book and had stopped at the casket, her hands gripping the velvet-covered rail, tears flooding her eyes. Now that she was closer, I could see that she wasn't Marilyn Monroe—she was a mess, all wrinkled and jumbled. The perfectionist in me wanted to get out the iron and the starch, maybe a lint roller, too, and straighten her out before sending her back out the door.

She was pretty, I'd give her that. Buxom and blond, the typical other woman. Except, I was a blonde, too. Just not so well endowed.

Had it been that simple? He'd needed some 36Ds to keep him company so he'd married another woman? My 34Bs weren't enough? I could have gotten a Miracle Bra, for God's sake.

Her diamond ring, the same shape as mine—apparently Dave hadn't been inventive enough to get something other than a marquise cut when he proposed a second time—sparkled in the muted light. Her mascara ran in dirty little rivers along her cheeks, and for a moment, I felt sorry for her. Had she known about me before today?

Had she loved him?

And would it really make a difference to me if she had?

She stepped back from the casket, but hesitated, clearly wondering if she should do the receiving line.

Always the polite girl I had learned to be, I stepped forward, reached for her hand. "I'm sorry," I said, before she could turn away or, worse, say it first.

Her eyes widened with surprise. "Me, too," she said softly. "I really am."

I wanted her to be some evil demon who'd stolen my husband with promises of chandelier sex and perfect Baked Alaska. But as I looked into her blue eyes—such a vibrant color compared to my own plain brown ones—I couldn't hate her. But damn it, I wanted to. It would have made the whole thing a lot more convenient.

"I didn't know," she said, taking a step closer, lowering her voice. "Not until I read the obituary in the paper."

I decided to believe her. If he'd fooled me for fifteen years, surely he could have fooled her, too. A hundred questions filled my mind. But then his mother was reaching for me, wanting to introduce me to some distant cousin I'd never see again, so I gave the other wife a slight, dismissive nod, and slipped back into the perfect portrait of what everyone expected of me.

Out of the corner of my eye, I saw her walk away, those crazy shoes sparkling in the muted light of the funeral parlor. We were members of the same club now, she and I.

I hoped like hell I wasn't going to find anyone else with a membership before this day was over.

CHAPTER 2

Somehow, I got through the wake without smearing Dave's good name or shrieking like a lunatic. My sister Georgia, Dave's brother Kevin, and Dave's mom were all there, keeping me company in the line beside the casket. That was it for family. My parents had died when I was seventeen, my grandparents shortly thereafter. Dave's father had passed away seven years ago from a heart attack, leaving Lillian to begin retirement as a widow.

I went home the night of the wake and cleaned a house that didn't need cleaning, organized closets that were already perfect and went through every pen in the house, scribbling the tips across an old magazine, looking for duds.

For something to do, to keep me from thinking.

At the funeral the next day, I did everything I was supposed to do. Laid a white rose on his casket before they lowered it into the ground, said thank you to everyone who offered their sympathies, turned down the offer of another casserole I wasn't going to eat. After a funeral dinner hosted by the ladies of the same church that had married and now buried my husband, I sent my sister home, telling her I would be okay. I thought of trying to talk to Dave's brother, to find out what he knew about this other woman, but right now, I wasn't strong enough to handle one more thing.

The other wife didn't show at the funeral and for an hour or so I pretended I was the only woman in Dave's life, that the words the pastor said about my late husband were true. "Good man...loving husband... devoted son."

At the end of the day, I slipped into the limo beside my mother-in-law to go back to the house Dave and I had bought a month ago.

The house where we were going to start a family.

He'd told me it would bring good luck, this change of residency. We'd been discussing the idea of kids for ten years, but I'd always had an excuse, a reason we should wait. I'd put him off and put him off, hoping that someday, Dave would just give up on the idea.

But then, finally, after Christmas, I had relented, finally conceding my fight to add anything more complicated than a potted plant to our lives. Because I was thirty-seven and Dave forty, we'd gotten checkups to make sure nothing was wrong. It wasn't his fault, the doctor had said. Dave had plenty of sperm to go around.

I stifled a laugh in the back of the limo. He'd had plenty of sperm to go around, all right.

My mother-in-law gave me a sharp glance, then let out a sigh. "Are you okay, Penny?"

"Yeah." *As fine as I'm ever going to be after coming face-to-face with my husband's extracurricular life.* "Lillian, if you want to stay at my house for a few days—"

"No. I'm going back to Florida, back home." She averted her face, watching the pastel tones of spring pass by the window. "I'm best going through this on my own. Do you understand, honey?"

She'd flown up as soon as I'd called her from the hospital and hadn't left my side since. I couldn't blame her for wanting some time away from this, to deal with her loss.

"Yeah. I feel the same way." Though I wanted to be alone for an entirely different reason, so I could sort out the mess of my husband's life and figure out how I could have been so easily duped by the same man whose underwear I had washed every Saturday. How could I have been handling those Fruit of the Looms and never realized he was a cheater? A bigamist?

A stranger?

I reached out and clasped Lillian's hand, giving it a squeeze. A tear ran down her face. She smiled at me, her eyes kind and worried. I'd always liked my mother-in-law, figuring I'd gotten awfully lucky to have married into a family where the normal jokes hadn't applied. Considering my own parents had been the dysfunctional poster children for how not to parent, I had latched on to Lillian soon after meeting Dave.

"Thanks for being here for me the last two days," I said. "I needed the support."

"I needed you just as much, dear," Lillian said, then sighed. "He's gone for both of us."

And for someone else. I bit my tongue. "He would have hated this, you know. The big funeral. The music."

"The flowers." Lillian laughed. "God, how Dave hated flowers at funerals. Said they were a waste of good landscaping plants."

I thought of the mums in our garage, the ones we'd planned on planting this weekend. He'd left me with a bunch of plants and a life half-done.

In the space of a day, my life had been thrown into a shredder, taking with it what I had hoped for my future, what I believed about my past, and what I thought I knew about my heart.

Talk about killing a whole bevy of birds with one stone. Dave's death had pretty much wiped out a species.

We pulled up in front of the house, the limo easing to a stop without even a squeak of the brakes.

Through the car's tinted windows, I saw her. Again. Like a bad nightmare I couldn't get rid of. Sitting on the swing—the swing Dave had installed last month—on my front porch, waiting.

"Who's that?" Lillian asked. "I don't think I saw her at the funeral."

"She's a good friend of Dave's." I didn't want to lie, but I couldn't tell anyone the whole truth. Not today. Maybe not ever. Heck, even I didn't want the whole truth.

"I'll let you two visit," Lillian said, giving me a final, comforting pat. "I want to go see Kevin again before I head to the airport."

Later, when I was ready, I'd corner Kevin and see what he knew. He and Dave had been close, going on annual fishing and hunting trips. He had to have told his older brother something.

Then as soon as I solved this mystery—and dealt with any financial ramifications—I'd bury it all in the back of my mind and get back to my predictable days.

It was the only way I knew how to deal.

I got out of the limo, said goodbye to Lillian, then strode up my walkway, not looking at the newly mulched beds waiting for plants. Ignoring the freshly painted white picket fence, the new front door. Projects we'd done last weekend. Apparently *my* weekend with him since the one before he'd been in "Toronto."

A fresh wave of pain slammed into my chest. Toronto, Denver, Dallas—how many of those trips had been lies? And to think I'd packed his suitcase, even throwing in a sexy note once in a while, and one time, a pair of my panties, because I felt bad for him attending those boring insurance conventions and client meetings.

I'd thought I was being so clever, such a perfect wife. Clearly, I hadn't, not if my husband had gone out and found himself a spare.

The other wife rose when I approached, still clutching that lace hanky. "I should have introduced myself," she said, extending a hand. "Susan Rey—" She cut herself off before giving me my own last name. "Susan."

Susan. It wasn't the name of a woman you could hate. It was one of those nice names, the kind given to the girl down the street who always let you play with her Barbies. She should have been named something else—Bambi, Cinnamon, Cassidy—something I could latch on to and despise.

"Penny," I said, shaking her hand and feeling weirdly like we were at a cocktail party, meeting for the first time over the crab dip.

"I know you probably have a million questions," Susan began, her voice filled with a nervous giggle.

I nodded. Actually, I thought a million was a low estimate.

"And I'd love to answer them," Susan said. She was neater today, more put together in jeans and a black top, but still with the same damned shoes. "But they'll have to wait."

"*Wait?* Why?" I wanted her to just tell me everything, to rip that Band-Aid off in one quick swoop.

Susan shifted on those heels and bit her lip. Her lipstick was darker than mine, I noticed, a shimmery cranberry compared to my muted coral. "Well…I have a favor to ask you," she said.

"A favor? You're asking *me* for a favor?" The whole day had become as surreal as a Jackson Pollock painting. I wanted to hit the wall, hit the mums, anything. Hit *her*, actually. "I want a favor, too. I want to know what you were doing with my husband."

"I can't—" She pressed a hand to her eyes, then

fluttered her fingers. "I can't talk about that right now. I need a little space. I just found out about you, too, you know. You have to give me some time."

I didn't want to feel sympathy for her. I wanted to hate her. Right now, anger was a lot more comfortable to wear than grief.

But damn it all, she had that nice name and big blue eyes and looked like the kind of woman I'd have coffee with. Not someone I could give a permanent placement on my shit list.

"Later, I promise," Susan said, and for some reason, I believed her. "But for now, I need you to take care of something for me. It'll be easy, I'm sure." She smiled, then stepped back and gestured into the shadows of my porch. When she did, I saw a cage.

It was small and tan, and filled with something that was so excited—or so vicious—it was shaking the plastic crate, causing it to tap-tap-tap on my wooden porch.

"What the hell *is* that?"

"Harvey the Wonder Dog," Susan said with a burst of enthusiasm, as if she'd just given me a long-awaited Christmas present. She backed down my stairs and onto my walkway. "And he's all yours."

"He's what? But—"

"I can't take care of him," Susan was saying, still

moving very fast, considering her shoes. "Dave had left him at my house while we went into the city and then…" She left off the rest. "Anyway, I've brought all his things. You'll love him. Really." Then she was reaching for the door of her black Benz, a car much like mine.

What had Dave done? Bought everything in pairs?

"Wait!" I shouted, barreling after her. "What are you doing?"

"Leaving." Susan withdrew a set of keys from her pocket and thumbed the remote. "Sorry."

"You're sorry… Sorry you married my husband? Sorry you showed up at his wake? Sorry you were on my porch, waiting for me to come home from burying him? Or sorry you dumped an animal on me that I don't want?"

Susan wheeled around, her hand on the door handle. "Sorry. But I've had him since Thursday and I can't take care of him anymore."

"He's your *dog*. Yours and Dave's," I said, the words thick as a turnip in my throat.

"No, he's not. I'm not even a dog person. He was Dave's. I never even met Harvey or knew Dave had a dog until Thursday. Now, he's yours." Susan let out a sigh. "Think of Harvey as a part of Dave, left to you."

Then, before I could ask her anything else, Susan had climbed inside her car, slammed it into gear and left, leaving me choking in her exhaust.

And apparently with one more member of the Dave Reynolds fan club.

CHAPTER 3

Harvey the Wonder Dog came with his own bed, a backpack of toys, his own special food and a rather vague set of notes, written in a six-by-nine composition book in Dave's tight scrawl.

The book had plenty of information about Harvey's tricks—balancing a beach ball on his nose while standing on his hind legs, barking the "Star Spangled Banner," complete with the high notes—and data on where he had appeared—*Letterman* twice, *Animal Planet* seven times, and *Good Morning America* once.

But not a word about why Dave had kept this circus side of himself, or the extra wife, secret. After Susan left, I brought the dog into the house, opened his crate to let him out, then sat down to read. Three hours later, I looked up to find Harvey the Wonder Dog still in his cage, shaking like a leaf, apparently not wonderful enough to conquer his fear of my kitchen.

How had he ever gotten up the gumption to appear on *Letterman*?

Then I remembered the note on page three. For every good deed he did, Harvey received a treat.

As I went to retrieve the bag of Beggin' Strips that had come with the dog, I wondered if that had been Dave's philosophy for everything. The new house, the tennis bracelet on my wrist, the love seat I'd admired in the showroom window of Newton Furniture—each thing bought after I'd done something that Dave decided needed a celebration. A new promotion, landing a big account—

Accepting his proposal of marriage.

I hated my husband right then, hated him as much as I had loved him. I felt the hatred boiling up inside of me, choking at my throat, begging for release. I wanted to tell him he'd screwed up my life but good by dying and then springing a secret existence on me at his funeral.

I didn't even *want* to think about what his dual marriage was going to do to our finances. To the life insurance, the 401(k) money. The house. Not to mention to my plans, my life.

"I hate you," I screamed at the walls. "I hate what you did. I hate how you left me. And I hate that you left me a dog instead of a goddamned explanation."

Harvey let out a bark and raised himself onto his hind paws, begging.

My sister, who'd always been a bit on the flaky side, would have said it was Dave's spirit, communicating through his canine counterpart to offer contrition. To me, it was a dog who'd spied the bag of treats in my hand and knew when to put on his sad face.

"Sorry, Harvey. I wasn't talking about you." I withdrew one from the package and waved it in Harvey's direction. "Here, puppy."

He bounded out of the crate, snatched the strip from my hand, then sat down in front of me, tail swishing against the floor. He didn't eat it, just held it between his teeth, his mouth spread so wide it looked as if he was grinning. His pointy brown-and-white ears stuck up, tuned to my every move.

"I don't know what to do with you," I said. "I've never even owned a dog, for Pete's sake."

Harvey wagged his tail some more.

"And I can't take you to…" I looked down at the book, flipping to the page of upcoming appearances, "the Dog-Gone-Good Show on Thursday. I have a job, you know, and it's not puppy chauffeur."

Harvey stretched his front paws across the floor, then laid his head down on them and let out a sigh.

The Beggin' Strip tumbled from his mouth and landed on the beige ceramic tile.

"I'm just going to have to find you a good home."

Harvey looked up at me, wide brown eyes in a tiny, triangular face, and waited. He wasn't an ugly dog, I reasoned. Why had Dave bought him? Trained him? Toured the country with him?

And most of all, why had he kept him secret?

A snippet of a conversation came back to my memory. Years ago, Dave had asked about getting a dog. I had turned him down, afraid that adding one more thing into my perfectly balanced life would make everything topple.

It was why I had gone into accounting. Nice straight lines, perfect columns of numbers. Everything adding up at the end.

Before I put one foot on the floor of my bedroom, I liked knowing what was coming each day and how the day was going to end. And yet, I wanted more. Wanted to have a taste of spontaneity, which was what had attracted me to Dave.

He was the Mutt to my Jeff, the Felix to my Oscar. I'd married him, thinking he'd help me loosen up a little, and he'd said he'd married me to keep him on track. But once we had the joint checking account and the mortgage to pay, it seemed those plans were dampened a bit.

I had liked our life just fine. Dave, clearly, had not.

The fact that I could have been so wrong hammered away at my temples. How could I have let details like this slip past me? What had I missed?

I looked again at the book, flipping back to the prior appearances page. Harvey had been at the Dog-Gone-Good Show last year. And the year before. Where had I been then? Where had I thought Dave had been? I tried to think back, but my mind was as jumbled as a bag of jelly beans. "Maybe there are some people there who knew Dave," I said aloud, talking to the dog, for God's sake. He barked, as if he agreed that it was about damned time I tried to sort this out and restore order.

He was right. If I was ever going to move past the shock of Dave's second wife—and his well-trained dog—I had to find out where things had gone so totally wrong. "I need to find some people who can give me some answers."

Harvey perked up, his ears cocking forward. His tail began again.

"And maybe I'm just nuts for talking to a dog about my cheating late husband." I tossed the book onto the sofa and crossed into the kitchen to pour myself a glass of wine.

The knock on my back door made me jump and nearly spill the Chardonnay. Through the glass oval I saw my sister. I groaned.

I love my sister Georgia, and though we've always been close, our personalities couldn't be more distant. We were as far apart as Venus and Earth. She's the Venus, I'm the Earth. Georgia believes in taking life as it comes, living by the seat of your pants and saving for retirement when you get over the hill, not while you're still climbing it.

The most spontaneous thing I ever did was buy Tide without a coupon.

I looked down at Harvey and realized I hadn't managed to avoid a damned thing.

"Hi," Georgia said, letting herself in. "I figured you could use some company tonight. I brought wine." She hoisted a bottle of Lambrusco.

I have told my sister at least seventeen times that drinking a sweet, full-bodied red is the equivalent of downing sugar straight from the box. Give me something dry, unadorned and I feel I'm actually having a drink.

Georgia never listened. She'd probably gone and

bought the bottle because it was the prettiest one in the aisle at the Blanchard's liquors.

Still, she was here, and no one else was. I had to appreciate her for trying. "Come on in," I said, gesturing inside. "And meet Harvey."

She halted inside the door, blinking at the Jack Russell terrier. "Harvey's a…dog."

"Dave's dog, to be precise."

"When did Dave get a dog?"

"According to his notes—2000."

Georgia's eyebrows knitted together. She laid the unopened wine bottle on the counter. "Notes?"

"It's a long story." I suddenly felt tired, so tired. I wanted to collapse onto the floor and stay there until a different day dawned. One without a dog looking at me expectantly, waiting for his road trip to Tennessee. One where everything was as regular as a clock and I didn't have to face a new question around every corner.

"Here," Georgia said, pressing me into a chair. "You look like hell." Once I was situated, she crossed to the counter, opened the Lambrusco and poured each of us a glass. I thought of protesting, but the energy to do it had left me a long time ago.

"Thanks," I said, and took a long swig of the wine, forcing myself not to gag.

"Harvey is Dave's dog," she repeated. "And he—"

She cut herself off. I looked at her face, noticed her staring at the dog, and turned my gaze to him. He was balancing on his hind legs, that silly Beggin' Strip on his nose. "And he does tricks," I finished.

"Oh my God," Georgia said. "I recognize him now. I saw him on the *Late Show* once. He's, like, famous."

"And now he's mine. Surprise, surprise."

Georgia ran a hand through her riot of blond curls. Last month, she'd had it straight and red. The month before, it had been black and spiky. I was surprised Georgia's hair hadn't mutinied. "Wait a minute. You didn't know Dave had a *dog?*"

"I didn't know a lot of things." I took a second swig of wine. A third. "Like that he also had another wife."

There. I'd said the words out loud. Now it was real.

All I had to do now was figure out a way to make it all go away.

Georgia opened her mouth, closed it, opened it again. "Another *wife?*"

"And apparently a road show with Harvey at the center." I shook my head. "I swear, I'm in *The Twilight Zone.*"

"What are you going to do?"

"Do?" I shrugged, then tipped the rest of the wine

into my mouth. "Go to work. Try to lead a normal life again. And find a home for Harvey."

At that, he slid back down onto the floor and let out a whine.

"You can't do that. He's like—" Georgia gave the canine an indulgent smile "—a lost spirit himself. He's been through a lot, too."

"He's also, like, a reminder of a husband who betrayed me," I said to Georgia, "then left me with a mortgage and a funeral bill I can't afford because God knows Dave was way too cavalier and happy-go-lucky to invest in something like long-term planning." I drew in a breath, tried not to choke on it. "Or a marriage."

Georgia let the heated words roll away. "But aren't you the tiniest bit curious? Like about why Dave did it?"

"No." I paused, finally listening to the thoughts and feelings that had been waiting behind Curtain Number Two in my head. "Okay, yes. I am."

"Then I say you investigate."

I shook my head, toying with the empty glass. "No. No way. I don't go running around, *investigating*. I go to work, pay my taxes and balance my checkbook. Like a normal American."

"Who happens to be married to a bigamist."

The word hung in the air, heavy, fat. I wanted to pluck it up and toss it away, bury it under the brown carpet I'd never liked but agreed to because Dave had thought it was homey.

I shook my head. "All I have to do is talk to Kevin. He and Dave were closer than anyone I know." Or at least, they'd seemed to be. Of course, I'd thought *I* was pretty close to my husband. But apparently knowing the man's inseam length and his favorite brand of shaving lather wasn't intimacy.

"What about the other wife? Did you meet her?"

"She was at the wake."

"She was?" Georgia let out a couple of curses. "Which one?"

"The one with the rhinestones on her shoes."

"Oh, those were cool shoes," Georgia said. "But on her, *totally* inappropriate."

I loved my sister for adding that, for saying the words she knew I was thinking.

"Did you talk to her?" Georgia asked.

"For about five seconds. She was here when I got home, but only stayed long enough to ditch the dog and run." I got to my feet, poured Chardonnay into my empty wineglass and returned to the table. "I don't know where she lives, and with a last name like Reynolds, I'll be banging on a thousand doors trying to find her."

Georgia thought for a minute, twirling the glass between her hands. "Did you check Dave's cell phone?"

Of course. He'd undoubtedly stored her number in there, probably with a voice tag, because he'd been incapable of dialing while he was behind the wheel.

"I got the feeling she doesn't want to talk," I said. "Besides, I'm not so sure I want to know what went on between her and Dave. I've had enough information to last me a lifetime."

"Have you asked the dog?"

"Asked the dog? Are you nuts? I can't talk to a dog."

"I bet Harvey is your key." Georgia nodded. "And I bet he knows a lot more than he's letting on with that little snout."

"I am not asking the dog. Or anyone on his upcoming six-city 'tour.'"

"He has a tour planned?" Georgia's turquoise contact colored eyes grew bright. "Perfect! I see a road trip in your future, sis."

"No, no, *no*." But even as I said the words, Georgia was off and running, retrieving the road atlas from the den.

"You have to do it, Penny," Georgia said. "Where's Harvey supposed to go first?"

"The Dog-Gone-Good Show in Tennessee in three days."

"How cool," Georgia said, flipping the pages, moving us visually toward Tennessee. "It could be the key to solving the greatest mystery of your life."

There'd been a reason I'd hated Nancy Drew books as a kid. I couldn't suffer through two hundred pages of mystery. I wanted to know the end before I began. I didn't want to take a path filled with unknowns. Dave was the one who would read Clive Cussler and Stephen King into the wee hours, who'd watch all eight weeks of an eight-week miniseries, content to wait a month and a half for the story's resolution. Me, I went for the *TV Guide* recap, the fast way to cut to the quick and eliminate anything extraneous.

I thought I'd lived my life the same way.

Until this week.

But as I sat in my kitchen, looking around at the sage-green room Dave and I had painted on a sunny afternoon last month, I realized I was living in a house filled with questions, not memories. There wasn't a corner of this house, a picture on the wall, that I could look at and not feel the doubts crowding in, jostling around in the spaces of my mind. Was any of it real? Or was I just clueless?

All I wanted to do was return to the life I'd recognized. Not run around the country with a dancing Jack Russell terrier, trying to figure out who Dave Reynolds had really been.

Even as I held back another round of tears, as reality slammed into me with the force of a nor'easter, I knew I had no choice but to start assembling this puzzle.

And the first place to start was with Susan.

CHAPTER 4

Susan Reynolds's phone number stared back at me in rounded tiny numbers, displayed on the tiny screen of Dave's Motorola phone. After my sister left and after two more glasses of Chardonnay, I'd finally gotten up the nerve to scroll through the listings in his phone book. I recognized only a handful.

What scared me was the names I didn't know. There was an Annie, a Kate, a Mindy. Two Pats—which could have been men or women—and a Matt. I'd stopped scrolling at the S's, too afraid to go farther. None of those names were familiar. They weren't people I'd met at the Greendale Insurance Company Christmas parties. They weren't names Dave had used in conversation.

I could, of course, call them and ask, *Uh, how did you know my husband? And did he tell you he was married to a Susan or a Penny?*

But no, I couldn't do that—not yet, anyway. I wanted the truth, but I also *didn't* want it, as if I could hold on to my fantasy that everything between Dave and I had been genuine.

Because if he'd duped me about being married, what else had been fake?

That was the real question I didn't want to answer. The one that clubbed my heart and broke it into smaller pieces every time I gave it voice.

I put the phone down, avoiding it to dig through drawers and filing cabinets, searching for Dave's will. I came up empty-handed and made a mental note to check his desk at work. Any man who was trying to hide multiple marital beneficiaries probably was smart enough to store that kind of evidence elsewhere.

Throughout it all, Harvey sat there and watched me, his little face jerking quickly with my every movement.

I found nothing. Not so much as a matchbook with a number scribbled on it. The only clues I had were in the Motorola.

I went back to the phone and scrolled through it again, leaving Susan down in the S's and went to Kevin. I hit Send, then waited for him to pick up.

"'Lo," he said. Behind him, I heard rock music playing in his bachelor apartment. Apparently Lillian was gone, because he had heavy metal going at full blast.

"Kevin, it's Penny."

"Oh, hi, Pen." His voice softened and he turned down the volume on his stereo. Kevin was the quiet one in the Reynolds family, who'd lacked the charm and sense of humor of Dave, but had the same studious way of watching someone while they talked, making them feel like the only person in the room. "How you holding up?"

"Fine. Ah, listen, I wanted to talk to you about Dave. About…well, what he did when he wasn't with me."

A pause. "I don't know anything about that, Pen. Sorry."

Across from me, Harvey started nosing at his little denim backpack, his name emblazoned in red glitter across the front. He pawed at it, then sat back and whined.

"You're his brother. You knew everything there was to know about him. You guys went everywhere together. Fishing, hunting, you name it."

"*I didn't go.*"

The words lingered between us, made raspy by the cell-phone static. There hadn't been an annual hunting trip to Wisconsin. Or the fishing trip to Maine each May. I'd never thought my husband was much of a sportsman, considering I was the one who baited the hooks at our lake vacation last August, but now I realized he hadn't been out looking for elk at all. He hadn't gone to any of the places he'd said he'd gone.

He'd been with *her*.

And Harvey.

It had all been a show. Another batch of lies. And Kevin had known, at least that Dave had been lying to me. The new betrayal slammed into me.

"I have to go, Kevin," I said, the nausea lurching up inside my throat again. I closed the phone and tossed it onto the sofa, not wanting to touch it—and the dozens of names I didn't know—for another second.

I curled into a chair and drew an afghan over my knees. The worn, multicolored blanket was as old as me, made by my grandmother when I'd been born, a blend of blues and pinks. I pulled its softness to my shoulders, then over my head, burrowing myself inside its comfort and darkness.

Here, the world was gone, quieted by the muffling weight of the thick, fuzzy yarn. Like I had throughout the rocky, tumultuous years of my childhood, I imagined staying right where I was until the worst was over. Harvey stuck his head under a corner, took one look at me and began wagging his tail.

The ringing of Dave's cell phone forced me out of my cocoon. I threw off the blanket and watched the

Motorola, its face lighting up in blue to announce the incoming call. For a moment, I hesitated, afraid to answer it. Afraid of who might be on the other end.

Eventually curiosity won out and I reached for the cell, flipping it open. "Hello?"

"Hey, is Dave there?" said a male voice I didn't recognize.

"No. He's…" I couldn't get the words out. I tried, even formed them with my lips, but they refused to be voiced. It wasn't *bigamy* I was afraid to say, it was *dead*. "He's gone right now. But I'm his wife. Can I help you?"

"You're Annie? Hey, cool to meet you. Dave talks about you all the time, you know."

Annie? Who the hell was Annie? A nickname for Susan? Or worse…

Another wife?

"Who did you say you were again?" I asked the voice.

"Oh, shit, I didn't introduce myself. I'm Vinny. I'm Harvey's trainer."

"Harvey's…trainer?"

"Well, hell, you didn't think he learned to dance and play the piano all by himself, did you?"

"He can play the piano?" I looked at the dog, sitting a few feet away, his tail swishing against the floor like a carpet clock.

"Not Mozart, but he can bang out a pretty good 'Twinkle, Twinkle Little Star.' That's what got him on *Good Morning America*."

I'd entered an alternate universe. Dave, a musically inclined dog and appearances on national television. Not to mention Susan and Annie. And whoever else I didn't know about.

"So, is Dave going to be at Dog-Gone-Good?" Vinny asked. "I was hoping he'd get here a couple days early so we can give Harvey a refresher on his dance routine. I tried calling Dave yesterday but he didn't pick up."

"He's…" I closed my eyes, took in a breath. "He died on Wednesday."

Silence on the other end, then an under-the-breath curse. "For real?"

"Yes."

"Aw, Annie, I'm sorry. He was a great guy. We're really going to miss him."

I pressed a hand to my stomach, as if putting a palm against my gut would give me strength I couldn't seem to find today. At least it would help me keep the soggy lasagna the church ladies made from making a return appearance. "And, my name isn't Annie," I said. "It's Penny."

A confused moment of silence. "But…but I thought you said you were his wife."

"I thought I was, too. Apparently I was sharing the job."

"Oh. *Oh.* Holy crap. Well, uh, I'm, ah, sorry." I could practically hear him fidgeting on the other side. "Listen, I gotta go. You, ah, take care. And if you want to send Harvey down to me, I'll make sure he does Dave proud at Dog-Gone-Good."

Before I could say anything else, Vinny was gone, leaving me with a phone that only seemed to quadruple the horror of my widowhood every time I went near it.

The pain of it all—of Dave's death, his betrayal, of the loss of my life as I knew it—ripped through me in a sob so big it tore through my throat.

"Oh, God," I cried, sobbing and yelling at the same time. I banged my fist against the carpet, then pulled back my stinging palm and pressed it against my chest, trying to hold my breaking heart in place.

Something wet and cold was on my hand, then on my face. I opened my eyes to find Harvey the Wonder Dog licking me, his tail wagging in ginger little movements, his ears perked like antennae, seeking, I supposed, signs of normalcy.

Harvey. Dave's legacy. What had Georgia called him?

The answer to all my questions.

Not much of an answer, considering he probably only weighed fourteen pounds soaking wet. But he was all I had, so I was starting there.

"Harvey," I said, swiping at my eyes, "want to go on a road trip?"

CHAPTER 5

To say Susan was surprised to see me on her Rhode Island doorstep the next morning would have been an understatement. She lived a little over an hour away from our house in Newton, in a small ranch with a magnolia in the front yard, which was starting to bloom in the bright early April sunshine.

When she saw me, Susan teetered on her high-heeled boots, enough that I thought she was going to faint. Then Harvey sprang out of my arms and into her house, and Susan recovered her wits.

"How did you find me?" she asked.

"Reverse lookup of your phone number in Dave's cell. The Internet is a dangerous thing."

She nodded, as if that all made sense, then opened her door wider. "Want to come in?"

"Actually," I said, drawing in a breath, "I want you to come out. And go to Tennessee with me."

She blinked. Behind her, Harvey was running in

circles around the perimeter of her braided rug, apparently seeing its endless oval as a challenge. "A road trip? To Tennessee?"

"Did you know about Annie?" I asked.

She thought a second, running the name through a mental phone book. "No."

"Well, it seems she might be Dave's wife, too. Meaning Mrs. Reynolds number three."

"He had another? Besides you and me?" Susan gripped the doorjamb. Now I really did think she was going to faint. I knew those feelings, having had them myself quite recently.

"Listen, why don't we sit down, have a drink and talk about it? I've already had time to digest this." I paused. "More or less. But I could still use a stiff one. Or two. Or ten."

Susan nodded, stepped back and turned to go down the hall, leaving me to follow. I shut the door, left Harvey to his circles and walked into Susan's bright yellow kitchen. It was a nice room, small but tidy, decorated in sunflowers and navy accents. The kind of kitchen I imagined a neighbor having. The kind of kitchen where I could see myself sitting down for a cup of coffee on a Thursday morning and gossiping about the guy across the street who mowed his lawn in his Speedo.

It wasn't, in other words, what I had expected from Dave's 36D wife.

"I have rum. And…tequila," she said, searching a cabinet above the Kenmore stove.

"Do you have Coke?"

She shook her head. "Diet Pepsi."

"It'll do." Heck, I would have had the rum straight, but I figured Susan didn't know me well enough to see me get drunk, something I'd done more in the past few days than in my entire life. After all that had happened, I was beginning to see the upside of staying perpetually toasted.

She poured two rum and Diet Pepsis over ice, then returned to the table, sliding one in front of me. Apparently Susan also wasn't paying attention to the clock when it came to having a respite from the shock and awe campaign executed by Dave's funeral.

I drank deeply, then pushed the glass away and folded my hands over each other. Susan was one of the keys to what had happened with Dave, to why he had married another. I needed her, even though I didn't want to.

"The way I see it," I began, "both of us have been screwed, pardon the pun, by Dave."

She nodded. Slowly.

"And I want to know why. I was married to him for fifteen years."

Susan raised a palm, wiggled her fingers. "Five here."

I swallowed that fact, allowing it to hit my stomach and churn in the empty pit with the rum. Five years. That meant he'd married her the year I was in the hospital having my appendix removed. I tried to think of when Dave had been gone then, but my brain had become a fuzzy mess of dates and lies.

For a second, I thought of telling Susan the whole thing was a huge mistake. Thanks for the rum, but I gotta go.

Then I realized leaving wasn't going to do anything but put me back to square one, and instead I stayed where I was, taking another gulp of my drink from a glass decorated with flowers around the edge, and tried to regain some kind of normalcy.

Ha. There wasn't any of that here. What I had was a whole lot of questions and a piano-playing dog who kept looking at me with expectant eyes, as if I was supposed to do some amazing trick, too.

"Well," I began again, trying to drum up the courage to press forward, to force myself out of the comfort zone where everything was a known quantity. "I don't know about you, but I want some answers."

Susan shook her head. "I—"

"Don't say you don't want to know." I waved the glass at her, the ice clinking in the emptiness. "Because you will. An hour from now, a day from now, you'll wonder *why.* You'll look in the closet and see his shoes—"

Oh, God, his shoes were under her bed, too. In her closet. Was this where his favorite blue shirt had gone? The one I'd torn the closet apart looking for last May? Or the yellow striped tie I told him I hated that he'd never worn again in my presence?

I clutched the glass tighter, to keep myself from running to her bedroom to peek and see how much of my husband was here.

"And you'll want to know," I went on, pushing the words past my lips, "because you're some kind of masochist who hates to have a mystery unsolved."

"I kind of like mysteries," Susan said, a bright smile on her face, as if I'd just handed her a new Nancy Drew.

"Work with me, Susan." I bit off the aggravation in my voice. "You can't tell me you don't want to know. About Annie. About where he went when he wasn't with you." I swallowed. "Or me."

She toyed with her still-full glass. Silence descended over the kitchen, seeming to darken the bright, pretty room. "I left him that day, you know."

"Yeah, the EMTs told me."

"We had a fight," she said.

I tried not to let on how much it weirdly pleased me to hear that he and Susan had had a fight.

"We had the fight after we…well, you know." A faint sheen of red filled her cheeks, a surprise in this woman who seemed so Manhattan. "Anyway, I left and took the train back to Rhode Island, figuring he'd catch up with me at home. If I had known—" Her voice caught on a sob and held the last syllable. "I'm sorry, Penny."

She was apologizing to me for leaving my husband. For not being there when he'd had a heart attack. She made it impossible to hate her. "I'm sorry for you, too."

She nodded, then picked up the tumbler, knocked back half the drink and slammed the small glass back onto the wooden surface. Brown liquid sloshed over the rim. "You're right. I want to know, damn it. I loved that man and I want some answers, too."

To hear her say she loved him hit me in the gut, hard. I rose, poured myself another drink—skipping the cola this time—and the feeling went away. A little.

Harvey the Wonder Dog trotted into the kitchen, his nose to the floor, looking for scraps, or maybe another rug to circle.

"I say we take him," I said, gesturing to the Jack

Russell terrier, "to this doggie show and ask everyone there about Dave. They knew him, they know Harvey."

"And if they won't tell us anything?"

I grinned at my strange new ally and raised my glass. "We'll break out the rum."

As she toasted my glass with her own, I had a flashing nightmare of the two of us ending up on *Jerry Springer,* telling our tale of woe while Harvey did tricks in the background.

Surely, it wouldn't come to that.

I'd go on *Oprah* before I'd ever sink to *Springer.*

Maybe.

CHAPTER 6

The next time I took a road trip to discover the truth about my late husband, I would go it alone.

Susan wasn't a bad person, but the combination of Harvey and her in the car nearly drove me over the edge. Susan chattering, Harvey pacing and whining. I was used to being alone in my car, listening to the music I liked, the talk-radio programs that interested me, but as we moved farther from Boston, the reception got worse and Susan's voice box revved up. She'd talked all through the night, making me regret letting her get a fifty-five-ounce Diet Coke at our last gas fill.

We'd stopped for fast food at one of the exits off of Route I-81 in Virginia. The place had been littered by ten million roadies before us, but Susan had assured me, one hand securely on my arm, that there couldn't possibly be any airborne viruses in a place like that.

Probably because they'd all run for the hills, overcome by the grease fumes.

I'd gotten a cheeseburger, but opted to have us eat in the car—breaking one of my cardinal rules—after I saw a fly groom himself on a table in the apple-themed food court.

"Here's a napkin," I said once we were back in the car. "You might want to spread it out, like a table-cloth. There are wet wipes in the glove box, so you don't get any grease on the door handles. Oh, and watch those little salt packets. They have a tendency to spray."

"Here, Harvey," Susan said, ignoring my housekeeping instructions and opening a six-piece box of chicken nuggets on the backseat of my Mercedes. Harvey dug in, as if he hadn't already had his shot of Purina for the day. His little jaws made quick work of the nuggets, spraying brown confetti crumbs over the leather.

"Can you get him to stop that?" I asked. "He's making a mess."

"He's a dog. He's allowed." Susan let out a sigh, her hundredth of the trip, then made a face at her window.

"This is a *Mercedes*," I said, realizing as I said it how pretentious it sounded. Like it was okay to get processed chicken tidbits all over a Chevy, but not a Benz. I relaxed my white-knuckled hold on the steering wheel, drew in a breath, let it out, then decided it was going to be a hell of a long drive to Tennessee if I didn't get a grip. "Never mind, I'm sure he'll eat all the crumbs."

He did just that, leaving a gooey white trail of doggy saliva on my seats in the process. Eww. I made a mental note to get the car reconditioned. Or better yet, call one of those crime-scene cleaners to erase all trace of dog.

The miles passed, with neither one of us talking. Harvey thrust his muzzle out the three inches of open window, sniffing the air with an enthusiasm that bordered on cocaine snorting. Every once in a while, he'd let out a yip, as if he'd seen someone he knew, his tail beating a greeting against the backseat. Then he'd hop down, dance around the backseat, nudge at his backpack, hop back onto the armrest and start the process all over again. If I hadn't known better, I'd swear he was doing doggy aerobics.

I switched on the radio, but couldn't get anything besides static. I watched the mile markers on I-81, which come every tenth of a mile, as if taunting me with how far I had yet to go, dread building in my stomach with each round number—261, 263, 268.

"Did you ever meet Vinny?" Bracing for the answer, I stiffened my spine and concentrated on the road— and not what lay at the end of it.

Because it sure as hell wasn't a leprechaun and a nice little pot of gold.

"Vinny?" Susan thought a minute. "No, though I heard Dave talking to someone with that name a couple times, if that helps."

A pang slammed into my chest, as sharp as a steak knife. Picturing Dave in her kitchen, or worse, her bedroom, sitting on the Sealy, lying against the pillows, talking on his cell. He'd have one ankle crossed over the opposite knee, and he'd be slumped a little, relaxed. If there was one thing Dave hadn't been, it was high-strung.

"Apparently, he's Harvey's trainer," I said.

"Oh."

In five seconds, conversation had died, may it rest in peace and never be resurrected. Had I really thought I could spend fifteen-plus hours in a car with a woman I didn't know, and had nothing in common with—

Except a husband.

Susan fidgeted beside me, adjusting the strap of her purse in her lap, then the deep V at her neck. Susan had a way of dressing that was just a step above street-walker and about five hundred steps away from me and my turtlenecks and St. John's Bay suit jacket. I wondered if that was what Dave had needed, a little dash of Victoria's Secret to keep my husband home. If I'd worn a V-neck instead of a turtleneck, would he have craved another woman?

I had to stop playing this guessing game. It certainly didn't improve my mood.

"So, Penny, what's the plan?" Susan asked me, pivoting in her seat as she did, her face now happy and bright, as if the whole thing was just oh-so exciting. Either she was putting on a good show because she was just as bored as I was, or she truly thought this was going to be one long pajama party.

"We go down to Tennessee, meet this Vinny, give him the dog and…" My voice trailed off.

"And find Annie?"

I turned and looked at Susan. "Do you *want* to find Annie?"

She sighed and, in that sound, I heard every emotion that had torn apart my heart in the past few days. Like it or not, the two of us were going through the same grieving, sharing the pain as if we were conjoined twins. "Not really. But I suppose we have to, don't we?"

I wanted to say no, we didn't. That we could leave Annie wherever she was in Podunk, USA, and go back to our merry lives like nothing had happened. That we could dump the dog and run.

But the practical side of me knew if there was a will—which I had yet to find in my search through the house—insurance money, social security death benefits, then there were legalities to work out between the three of us. *If* there were three. Maybe Annie was Harvey's breeder or dog food provider or something.

"This is kind of fun," Susan said, resting one skinny bare arm on the door. "I've never been on a road trip before."

Fun? She was having *fun*?

"I haven't traveled much, either."

"Why not? You seem the…sophisticated type."

"I'm an accountant," I said, as if that was an explanation for everything.

"But don't you have, like, accountant get-togethers where you discuss exciting things about taxes or whatever?"

I laughed, the sound bursting from my lungs so spontaneously I almost didn't recognize it. It had been days since I'd laughed. Weeks, maybe. "Well, they do have conferences, but I've only been to one."

"Why?"

"I don't do well in strange places."

"Oh."

"I mean," I hastened to add, in case it sounded as if I was some kind of an agoraphobic conference freak, "that a conference throws me off my schedule."

"I don't even own a watch," Susan said, as if that should make total sense to me.

In a weird way, it did.

In the beginning of our marriage, Dave had asked me to travel, to go with him to conventions and client appointments in different cities. I'd tried it, once, and found the whole experience so unnerving and so out of my control that I'd never gone again. I'd pleaded headaches, the flu, work deadlines—until Dave stopped asking.

Now I knew why. It hadn't just been my reluctance that had made him quit inviting me along. He'd been hiding a life that he'd apparently decided I didn't want to share.

If he'd asked one more time? If he'd told me...

What would I have said?

I already knew that answer. Hell no, I didn't want a dog that could pirouette. And a definite nix on the idea of trotting him around dog shows all over the country. I mean, we'd had a mortgage to pay, a lawn to mow, for Pete's sake.

"Oh, look, hitchhikers!" Susan pointed at what was clearly a novelty to her, standing on the highway in the misty rain. "Let's stop."

"Haven't you read Stephen King? Don't you know the chances of us being maimed or robbed...or worse?"

Susan waved a hand in dismissal. "Oh, they look okay."

I glanced at the couple by the side of the road as we neared them. A scrawny guy in jeans with long, unkempt brown hair standing beside a short, plump woman who was either pregnant or hiding an Uzi under her shirt. "No. We're not picking them up."

"Fine." Susan pouted, then turned her face again toward the window, giving the couple a little wave as we drove past.

Mile marker 274. Tennessee had never seemed so far away.

If these miles didn't start passing faster, or if Susan didn't suddenly fall asleep in her seat, there was going to be a felony committed in this car. And it wouldn't be at the hands of some nameless hitchhiker.

"Susan, listen, I—"

The Benz jerked to the right with a loud pop, cutting off my sentence. I gripped the wheel, struggling to pull the car back into the lane before we were creamed by a mint-green Honda Odyssey puttering along in the slow lane.

"Holy crap! What just happened?" Susan asked, her face deathly white.

"Flat tire." Or at least, that's what I assumed. I'd never had anything go wrong with the Benz. Dave had always taken care of maintenance and when one car wore out, he'd replaced it with another just like it, black, dependable. "I think."

I slowed, waited for the Odyssey to go by, then pulled off the road, gravel spitting between my tires and dinging against the body. The Benz leaned to one side, sinking into the ground as if an elephant had taken over Susan's spot.

I got out and walked around to the front of the car, feeling the whoosh of traffic passing by, lifting my hair and jacket, making them flap in the hurried sixty-five-miles-per-hour breeze. There was no mistaking what had happened. The tire on the passenger side had gone flatter than a sheet of cardboard.

"Do you know how to fix it?" Susan asked, climbing out of the car and standing beside me in her ridiculous heels, shoes that were definitely not designed for performing car maintenance.

"No. I know how to call Triple A, though."

Susan looked disappointed, as if she'd paid her dollar for an adventure and was expecting me to provide one. I went back to the car, searching for my cell phone. It wasn't in the ashtray/change dish. Not in the cup holder, not on the dash, not in my purse. I started feeling blindly along the carpet, trying to ignore the French fry and nugget crumbs, then finally found it. Under Susan's seat, the cover flipped open.

The battery was dead.

When had I gotten this distracted that I'd forget to recharge my cell? That I hadn't even noticed it had bounced out of my purse? I couldn't think of a single other time when I hadn't been on top of everything, knowing exactly how to get from A to B.

And yet, I'd left this morning in a car with a woman who was a total stranger with nothing more than an overnight bag, a road atlas and a can of soda. I'd never done anything that unrehearsed, that unplanned.

At least not until my dearly beloved and stone-cold husband had thrown a big old roadblock into my life. A roadblock with impossible shoes and a tendency to talk at the worst time.

I cursed and tossed the useless cell onto the seat. It hit the hard surface of the armrest, bounced up and pinged into the backseat. Harvey let out a yip, then cowered in the corner.

And peed on the leather.

That was it. The last straw in a haystack that was already depleted. I started to cry, collapsing onto the driver's seat in a useless heap. What was I thinking, driving this far? I could have just stayed in Newton, handing off the estate to some attorney who would tell Susan and Annie they'd get to split the dog and none of the things Dave and I had worked so hard to build together.

I didn't want to hear that our entire life had been a group effort, that I had to triangulate my assets, as I had my husband.

Soon as the tire was fixed, I was turning around, heading back home. I didn't want to know what Dave had been up to. I didn't want his damned dog. And I especially didn't want his other damned wife.

"Penny?" Susan's touch was light on my shoulder. "You okay?"

"Yes." Years of conditioning, of pretending everything was all right even as it crumpled around me, spit that word out on a sob.

"Don't worry about the tire. Help has arrived." She

gestured beside her with a flourish, at the two hitch-hikers I'd bypassed five minutes earlier.

They grinned at me. I gave them a watery, please-don't-rob-us-and-leave-us-to-die-here smile back.

Somehow, given the circumstances lately, I had a feeling my luck wouldn't be that good.

CHAPTER 7

It turned out Norm, the scrawny guy, knew how to change a tire and pop off a wheel cover, but lacked the strength to get the lug nuts off, so he had his girlfriend stand on the tire iron. Apparently neither one of them cared that she was six months pregnant—something Norm proudly told me as his girlfriend lifted up her Penn State sweatshirt and displayed a big round belly with an outie that seemed a lot like a tongue sticking out at us.

"Are you sure she should be standing on that?" I asked Norm. I had finished cleaning the seat with the wet wipes, given Harvey the evil eye, then swiped the whole thing down again with the remaining napkins. What I wouldn't have given for a little Lysol.

He shrugged. "Rita's cool with it. Aren't ya, baby?"

She beamed at him and gave the metal rod a little bounce. "Absolutely. I do it all the time in the garage where Norm used to work."

"Where are you guys headed?" Susan asked after the

kid—the closer I looked the more I realized Norm couldn't be a day over seventeen—finished jacking up, replacing, then jacking down.

"Dollywood," his girlfriend answered for him. "Norm's a country singer. A real good one, too. We're headed there for this season's *American Idol* tryouts. Norm's gonna be a *star*."

Her smile for him was so filled with adoration and hope that I didn't have the heart to mention Norm's chances of breaking onto the Billboard Top 100 were about nil. Particularly since he looked more like Charles Manson's younger brother than Clint Black's replacement.

"You're all set," Norm said. He swiped his greasy palms across his jeans, then stared at me expectantly.

"Uh… How much do you want?" I said, reaching for my purse, keeping it hidden behind the open door in case Norm and Rita got any ideas.

"Nothin'," Rita popped in. "'Cept maybe a ride. Susan says you guys are going to Tennessee, too."

I shot Susan a glare, but she ignored me. "We really can't—"

"Get on in," Susan said, ignoring me. "We could definitely use the company."

Which meant she wasn't having much more fun

than I was. I said a quick prayer that neither one of them was a homicidal maniac, then slipped in behind the wheel. I did owe Norm, after all.

I pulled out onto the highway, easing into traffic, giving the tire a test before getting back up to full speed. Behind me, Harvey settled in between the two new passengers, sitting up and panting something that looked oddly like a smile.

"Oh my God!" Rita shrieked.

"What? What?" I whipped my head around, trying to ease across two lanes, back to the side of the road. Was she in labor? Had the wheel slipped off? Had Norm forgotten to reattach the lug nuts?

"It's that dog, baby," she said, smacking Norm on the arm, making his faux leather jacket crinkle. "The one from *Letterman*."

Norm leaned around to look at Harvey head-on. "Holy crap, it is. Harry the Dog."

"Not Harry, silly. *Harvey* the Wonder Dog."

At that, Harvey let out a yip of agreement. He sat up and begged, then did a twirl of a dance around the leather. I thanked God that he didn't get *too* excited. I only had so many wet wipes.

"You own Harvey?" Norm asked, clearly impressed. I could have been Dolly Parton for all the awe I saw reflected in my rearview mirror. "That's, like, cool, dude."

"I only sort of own him." I concentrated on getting the car back on the road, without being creamed by a passing double semi.

"Oh, Penny, don't be so modest," Susan said. "She's Harvey's mommy."

Only because you dumped him on me, I thought but didn't say. "We're both his owners," I said, giving Susan a friendly you're-stuck-with-me-in-this-one smile.

"Dude, this dog is, like, famous." Norm let out a low whistle. "No wonder you're driving an M.B."

"M.B.?" I said.

"Mercedes-Benz, dude. A rich chick's car."

I wasn't rich, nor was I a chick, but I let it go. The green sign on my right promised the Tennessee state line was only another forty miles away. Pigeon Forge was another thirty from there. Soon, Norm and Rita would be gone, off to pursue fame and fortune at Dollywood.

Or maybe just ride the rides and leave with their ticket stubs and some disappointment.

"So, like, what kinda tricks can you make him do? Can you get him to do that thing where he opens a can? Man, if he could pop open a brewski, he'd be a damned handy dog." Norm thought a second. "Though, it might be better if he could open the fridge *and* the brewski. Save me from getting off the couch."

I didn't say anything about his obvious underage status and the fact that he was already sofa surfing and drinking beer. Not to mention the example he'd be setting for his future child.

"So, what can you get him to do?" Norm asked again.

"*Hello,*" I said, annoyed and frustrated with my passengers, "I'm not really his—"

I caught sight of Harvey in the rearview mirror. He was standing on his back paws again, waving the two others at me.

"Cool. He waves."

I'd said hello, the dog had started to wave. Coincidence or was Harvey listening to me? I opted for the first one.

"He's such a cutie," Rita said. "Do you know how old he is?"

"How old are you, Harvey?" I asked, half joking, figuring the dog would ignore me and go back to his crumb hunt. Instead, Harvey began pawing at the seat, almost tapping on it. Once, twice, three times… eight times total. "Eight," I said, not sure I'd just seen the dog count, but maybe…

I mean, he *was* called Harvey the Wonder Dog. Wouldn't he at least be able to tell how old he was? Dave had mentioned a few tricks in the journal, but overall he'd been pretty vague, mentioning things like Harvey's A Routine and his C Routine, whatever those meant. Either way, it didn't matter to me. Soon enough, Harvey—and his routines—would be Vinny's problem.

"Oh my God!" Rita shrieked a second time.

"Don't tell me that dog peed again." My wet wipe supply was running low, along with my patience.

"Uh…no." In the rearview mirror I saw Norm's eyes grow wide as Rita began to curse and yell, grabbing at his hand. He held hers tight, their joined knuckles turning white, along with every feature in Norm's face. "We gotta go to the hospital. I think Rita's having the baby."

At that she let out another scream and smacked him with her other hand. "Will you quit talking and just get this thing out of me?" She whipped her head around, glaring at Norm. "This is all your fault, you—"

Another scream, a third smack-down for the situation. Norm took it all, no complaint, but the color was a shade off in his face. "*Dude,* we gotta go faster."

"You said she was only six months pregnant." I swerved again, into the exit lane, narrowly avoiding a FedEx truck. My gaze darted to the roadside, praying for a little blue sign with an H.

Norm shrugged, cool as a cucumber. "What do I know? I failed math three times."

CHAPTER 8

Pandemonium.

That word pretty much summed up the entire day. In Whitfield, we found a hospital, thank God, and brought in Norm and a nonstop screaming Rita. By the time we got there, she was full out thrashing and clutching at Norm and begging for drugs. I started calculating the chances she'd give birth on my backseat.

Not even Johnson & Johnson had enough wet wipes to cover that kind of mess. And I doubted Harvey's skills extended to midwifery.

In the end, the leather was saved, the tire held and Rita turned out to be having a hell of a bad case of Braxton Hicks. The hospital kept her overnight for observation.

"You can't be hitchhiking with her," I told Norm in the hall, feeling like the housemom for Dropout U. Susan was inside Rita's room, the two of them laughing and giggling, as if this had just been one more adventure.

Norm lifted one shoulder, then dropped it. "I gotta get my chance at Hollywood, dude. Rita'll be cool."

"Do you want your future son or daughter born on the highway? You need to get her home. Think of the baby, not yourself."

"Dude, it's *American Idol*. It's like the biggest show on TV. If I go home now, I may never get my shot." Norm toed at the floor, streaking black rubber across the pristine vinyl. "Besides, we ain't got no place to go home to. Rita's dad kinda blames me for her…condition."

"Well, you did get her pregnant."

"Yeah, but I, like, love her and everything." He looked back at the room. His gaze softened and in it, I did see love, or at least I thought I did. I wasn't sure anymore if I could read a man's expression and know what he was really thinking. "I was gonna get a job, get us a place to crash, but Rita, she really wanted me to do this singing thing. She says I got charisma."

He had something, that was for sure, because Rita saw the sun and the moon in his face. And whenever they were alone, I'd noticed he reflected that solar system right back at her.

I dug in my purse and pulled out the cash I'd withdrawn that morning. It was only a few hundred dollars, but I hoped it would be enough for the two of them to get back to their homes and some sanity. "Take this," I said, handing it to Norm. "Go home, find a place, a job, some baby furniture. Promise me you'll marry her. And keep it to one wife."

Norm's eyes grew wide. "That's, like, a lot of money. I only changed your tire."

"Be good to her. Talk to her and be smart about your decisions." I left off the rest of the lecture that had been stewing in the back of my mind. Who was I, the Clueless Wife, to tell Norm and Rita what to do?

"Thanks. You're, like, a chick with heart," Norm said, closing his hand over mine, then releasing it to give me what I thought was a peace sign. "Keep it posi, dude. And good luck with Harvey."

"Yeah, thanks." I probably needed the luck more than Norm, who seemed oddly grounded and cool about the direction his life had taken. I grabbed Susan and we left, stopping by the hospital ATM on the way.

"I saw what you did," Susan said.

"I didn't want them holding up a minimart to pay for a crib."

Susan laughed, then wrapped her arms around me in a hug.

I cleared my throat and pulled back. "We have to

get Harvey to the dog show before he eats my dash-board."

Susan kept up her usual chatter during the hour and a half it took us to reach Pigeon Forge and then the Grand Resort Hotel and Convention Center that was hosting the Dog-Gone-Good Show. She talked mainly about Norm and Rita, about their baby, about Norm's singing voice and how his audition would go. I tried to respond but barely got more than a word or two in.

When Susan's motor was started, there was no stopping it. I was actually relieved to park the car at the hotel and enter a whole new kind of crazy.

Harvey bounded out of the car the second I opened my door, ran through the lobby, past the bellhop's attempt to grab him and straight into the Dog-Gone-Good registration fray. "Harvey!"

He ignored me and kept on going, weaving his little body in and out among the other dog owners and their pooches. He nearly missed being sideswiped by a Lab-radoodle, darted under a Great Dane as if it was a bridge, and skidded to a stop before the skirted table, leaping up onto the white surface and wiggling his way toward the third man on the right.

Around me, I heard people calling out Harvey's

name, telling each other the Wonder Dog was here, laughing at his break for freedom. People pointed, smiled, waved at the terrier.

Harvey, apparently, was a regular celebrity on the dog-show circuit.

"Harvey!" I screamed, mortified. Stupid dog, why couldn't he obey? Wasn't that what he was trained to do? And where the heck was a Beggin' Strip when I really needed one?

"Harvey!" the man cried, wrapping his arms around the dog and submitting to the terrier's wild tongue introduction. "Where you been, buddy?"

I made my way through the crowds, reached forward and snapped Harvey's leash onto his collar. "I'm sorry. He got away from me."

The man grinned. "Once Harvey gets an idea in his head, he goes after it. The only time you can get him to behave is on the stage."

I studied the man in front of me. Not a bad-looking man at that. Dark hair with a dusting of gray, tall, reasonably well built. Green eyes that were just a shade above gray. No one I'd ever met before, but that didn't surprise me. Dave had clearly kept this entire side of his life a secret. "How do you know Harvey? Are you his trainer?"

"I'm his agent."

A woman slipped into the line beside me, carrying a white poodle whose froufrou hairstyle had been jazzed up with hot pink bows. She was cooing to the dog, telling it everything would be just fine. Cee-Cee, the dog, quivered in the woman's arms, as though she was about to pee. I stepped a little to the left, keeping my Rockports out of Cee-Cee's aim.

"Harvey has an *agent?*" I said.

The man chuckled. "Hell, ninety percent of the dogs here do. And those that don't are looking to chomp on to the first one who shows an interest."

"Dave never—" Dave hadn't mentioned an agent in the journal for Harvey, but I didn't want to tell this guy that. Maybe they'd been on the outs? Maybe Dave hadn't seen it as an important detail?

Or maybe the guy was making the entire thing up.

"Matt Shay," he said, thrusting out his hand. I recognized the name from Dave's cell directory. Success.

"Penny Reynolds," I replied, shaking with him. He had a firm grip, the kind that said he was comfortable in his own skin, in the jeans and button-down shirt he wore.

"Are you related to Dave?"

"I'm his wife."

I had to give the man credit, he didn't blink an eye. Didn't betray his surprise at all. "Penny. That's right, he's mentioned you."

I didn't want to call his bluff. I didn't want to make him admit that he'd never heard of me before. That the woman Dave had called his wife had been Annie or Susan or worse…someone else. "Nice to meet you."

"Vinny told me Dave had…passed away," Matt said, drawing Harvey closer to his chest and absently fingering the dog's ears. "I'm really sorry."

The crowd pressed in against me, people shouting out their dog's FAQs, their addresses, phone numbers, screaming names like "Sir Hightower Golden Fancy" and "Lady's Lost Slipper Deluxe."

I nodded, swallowing back the lump in my throat. "It was pretty sudden."

"What happened?" Then he put up a hand. "No, no. You don't have to talk about it."

Good. Because I had no intention of telling this stranger, the dog's agent, for God's sake, that my husband had been found dead after screwing his second wife. A wife who was finally bringing up the rear, after a prolonged trip to "the little girls' room."

"Penny! There you are. You won't believe it. They have *dog biscuits* in the ladies' room. In the little—"

Susan cupped her hand over her mouth "—candy machine, if you know what—" She stopped talking when she noticed Matt. "Hello. I'm Susan Reynolds."

"Matt Shay," he said, shaking with her, too. "You must be Dave's sister."

Susan laughed. "Oh no. I'm his wife."

Matt's mouth dropped open. I wanted to die right there, sink into a hole in the floor and take Susan with me.

Susan and I hadn't thought to discuss this. All those hours in the car and the whole "what do we say when people ask" question had never come up. I guess I'd just assumed Susan would let me be the wife and she'd play Dave's friend.

Susan covered her mouth as if she'd just realized what she'd said. "Well, Dave was a busy guy," she said, with one of those little laughs of hers.

Cee-Cee's owner turned around and stared at us. She elbowed the woman behind her. "Lucy, did you hear that? They're one of them polygamy families," she whispered, in decibels they could hear in space. "Bunch of perverts."

"This was a bad idea," I said, taking Harvey out of Matt's arms, with a protest from the dog, and wheeling around. I hadn't thought about how we'd answer these questions, how I would deal with what people would think. I'd been intent on getting here, ridding myself of the dog and determining how far I'd have to split Dave's assets. My plan lacked…a plan.

Ignoring the stares and whispers, I wove my way quickly through the crowd, my eyes fixed firmly on the four red letters of *Exit*.

Go home. Go back to normalcy. Pretend all of this never happened.

"Penny!"

I ignored Matt's voice and plunged forward, through a crowd of collies, their owners looking as poufy as the dogs themselves. A weird part of my mind, the part that had completely disassociated from this entire surreal experience, wondered if they'd be called a crowd. Or a litter. Or a bark, or some other weird thing. Tears rose to my eyes—when had I become this weepy creature? I never cried—and I stumbled into a group of poodles, the leather straps wrapping around my legs and tangling my steps.

"Penny," Matt said, reaching for me across the over-groomed white dogs. "What's wrong?"

I stepped back, out of the leashes, and kept backing up until I hit the solidity of a column. "Come on, Matt. Tell me you aren't that clueless."

"Actually, I am." He grinned. "It's part of my DNA, or so my ex-wife told me."

I couldn't help but laugh, the kind of relieved laugh you let out when you've narrowly missed creaming the neighbor's bushes because a chipmunk ran in front of the car. I sobered when I caught a glimpse of Susan stuck on the other side of the dog pool, waving at me like a mariner lost at sea. "I think it's pretty obvious. I'm Dave's wife and so is she."

He shrugged. "That's okay. I mean, I've heard about those kind of arrangements, but never—"

"It is *not* that kind of arrangement!" I forced myself to lower my voice when several people turned to stare. "I never knew he had another wife."

"Until after he—"

"Yeah."

"Oh." His eyes grew rounder. "That must have been horrible."

"You know, this isn't my favorite topic of conversation. I came down here to give Harvey to you or Vinny or whoever's in charge because I don't want a dog, I don't want to go to the Dog-Gone-Good Show and I don't want—"

And then I was crying again.

"Hey, hey," Matt said, coming closer to me, taking

my arm. "It's okay. It'll work out. Come on, let me buy you some coffee."

"But what about the show and Susan and—"

"I think you need a cup of coffee more than any of those things need to be handled." Still holding my arm, he gently led me out of the room, through a back door in the ballroom. Immediately, the crazy zoo behind us was silenced. Five minutes later, we'd left the building by a side entrance that kept us far from the registration fray.

As I thought of all the questions I needed to ask Susan—questions I still wasn't a hundred-percent sure I wanted to know the answers to—I wondered if it might be less painful to just take a bath in gravy and offer myself up as a lobby sacrifice.

CHAPTER 9

I don't know what kind of man I expected a dog agent to be, but it wasn't Matt Shay.

"Hey, Matt, you escaping again?" the redheaded, statuesque waitress said as she led us to a booth in the back of a diner named The NightOwl. Situated down the street from the Grand Resort Hotel and Convention Center hosting the Dog-Gone-Good Show, it was one of those retro buildings made to look like an old-fashioned railroad dining car.

Most of the customers were males over the age of sixty, debating sports stats along with the talking heads on ESPN, which played on every TV in the diner except for one in the back running cartoons. No children were watching "Tom and Jerry," but one middle-aged guy was, sitting to the right of the set and laughing as if Tom the cat had the comedic ability of Robin Williams.

"Thanks, Lucille," Matt said as he slid into the

booth. The waitress didn't bat an eye at Harvey, who slipped onto the seat beside Matt and promptly fell asleep, apparently tuckered out from watching me do all the driving. "Bring me some high-octane coffee and for my guest…" He looked to me.

"A cup of the same. Leave plenty of room for cream, please."

"Good," he said, smiling, after Lucille left.

I realigned the salt and pepper, putting them squarely against the silver napkin holder. "What's good?"

"You're not one of those cappuccino women."

"What's a cappuccino woman?"

"You know, the kind that goes into Starbucks and orders a coffee like she's picking out a car? Tall, noncaf, nonfat, venti mocha with a double sugar-free caramel shot." Matt rolled his eyes. "Get a damned coffee, not a short story."

I laughed. "I can honestly say that I am probably the only person on the planet who has never stepped foot in a Starbucks."

He put out his hand and shook mine again. "Meet the only other one."

I laughed again. At this rate, it was becoming a habit. "What's good here?" I asked, feeling a wave of guilt that I was laughing when my life was such a shambles. I was a widow, for God's sake. I shouldn't be laughing at another man's jokes.

I jerked a menu out of the metal holder and scanned the diner's offerings, instead of the man across from me. My stomach rumbled, which reminded me I hadn't eaten in hours, not since we'd done that live-action version of "A Baby Story" with Norm and Rita.

And Susan. Oh, no, I'd ditched her, without a thought.

"Everything's good here. Willhemina, the owner, makes everything from scratch, the way her mother and her mother's mother taught her. Which means this isn't the kind of place where you watch your calories or your cholesterol." Matt's gaze ran over my face. "You worried about Susan?"

"Yeah." I put the menu to the side and glanced out the window. "I shouldn't have left her there."

He flipped out a cell phone, punched in a number, then waited as the call connected. "Jerry. Look for a tall blonde in a black minidress and—"

"Red shoes with rhinestones," I supplied.

"Red shoes with rhinestones." He paused. "I should have known you'd find her before I could get past the word *blonde*." Matt chuckled, a nice, hearty male sound. "Tell her Penny and I are grabbing a bite to eat and we'll be back." He paused, laughed some more. "Okay. Sounds good." He closed the phone and tucked it back into his pocket.

"What sounds good?"

"Jerry offered, out of the kindness of his heart, I'm sure, to keep Susan entertained. He's got a weakness for blondes." Matt grinned. "I have a feeling you won't see Susan for a while. Jerry'll whisk her off on a tour of the city or something."

Relief settled over my shoulders, displacing the heavy weight of worry. For a while, I could forget about Dave's other wife. Have a meal and a conversation and pretend everything was fine. For now. "Thanks."

He shrugged. "Hey, we're a full-service agency."

I laughed again, then thanked Lucille as she deposited two cups of coffee before us, along with a generous handful of creamers.

"Where's Vinny?" I asked, laying my napkin on my lap and smoothing it into place.

"Harvey's trainer? Oh, he usually doesn't do these kinds of things. He's not good in a crowd."

"But isn't he the one who takes Harvey onstage?"

"Yeah, when we can get him sufficiently liquored up and convinced he won't die." At my knitted brow,

Matt leaned forward and lowered his voice. "Vinny has a bit of stage fright."

"But he'll be fine at the Dog-Gone-Good, right?" Suddenly, I wanted Harvey to succeed, to do as well as he had in the past. The part of me that still loved Dave knew he had loved that stupid dog, and had invested a lot in his success.

"Yeah, I'm sure he will." But Matt didn't sound so confident. "Vinny'll get over his little problem between now and Tuesday."

"Little problem?"

"He, ah, breaks out in hives whenever he has to get near a stage. He had a bad experience with Rin Tin Tin the second six months ago and ever since then, he gets a little nervous."

"A little?"

"Okay, a lot. And the hives are…well, they're more like facial explosions. The makeup artist on *Letterman* had to use a paint sprayer to cover them."

That sounded like a lot more than a small problem. I fiddled with my silverware, aligning it, one bottom edge perfectly against the other. "Can't you do it?"

Matt shook his head. "Harvey's particular about who he listens to. Apparently I'm not on his friends-and-family list."

"But he likes you so much."

"Harvey likes everyone. He doesn't obey everyone, though. He's a star, so he tends to be temperamental."

I slid a piece of ice into my mouth and toyed with it, before crunching the cube and swallowing. My dentist would have been appalled, but I figured if the worst thing I did right now was start chewing ice, then I'd take the tsk-tsk from Dr. Diehl.

Harvey had awakened and slid under the table, then up onto the vinyl seat beside me. He wagged his tail, prancing on the seat and watching me expectantly, probably thinking I had a few Beggin' Strips in my purse. "Sit, Harvey," I said. He did, tamping his enthusiasm a bit.

"Have *you* tried working with him?" Matt asked.

"Me? No, no. Not at all."

"He likes you." Matt gestured toward the dog with his fork. "And he seems to behave for you, too."

I thought of the car ride and how Harvey had tapped out his age, or at least what I presumed was his age. How he'd sat when I'd told him to, stayed when I asked him to. Not to mention that whole thing with waving hello. *Was* he listening to me? "Are you suggesting what I think you are?"

Matt grinned, the kind of smile that normally

would have had me thinking he liked me, that there was something more than a conversation about a dog going on here. "Only if you're considering it."

"No. No, no, *no*. I will not go onstage with the dog."

"It's an easy job. Harvey does all the work."

At that, Harvey let out a yip of agreement, then did his turnaround dance on the seat.

I hadn't driven all this way to end up onstage with a dog I didn't even want. I was here for answers, not my shot—or rather Harvey's shot—at fifteen minutes of fame. "I'm an accountant, for God's sake."

Matt grinned. "All the more reason to step out of your comfort zone."

I dug in my purse, found a few ones and threw them at the table, then rose. "You don't understand. This entire trip has been out of my comfort zone. My marriage, it turns out, wasn't even on the same *planet* as my comfort zone. I'm not taking that dog onto a stage or in front of a camera or anywhere else for that matter. You're his agent, you deal with him."

Then I turned and walked out of the diner, leaving Harvey the Wonder Dog, and his wonder agent behind. I'd done half of what I came here to do.

The easy half, my mind whispered. Dealing with

Annie—and who she was or wasn't—was going to be a lot harder than leaving a dog in a diner.

"There you are!" Susan exclaimed, coming up to me the second I hit the sidewalk. She was trailed by a man about five years younger than she, who was all puppy-dog eyes and clear infatuation with the statuesque, busty blonde. "I've been looking all over for you."

"And I was on my way to find you. We need to—"

Before I could say "go home," Susan grabbed my arm, her eyes bright with excitement, and dropped a bombshell in my lap. "I found Annie," Susan said. "And you'll never believe what I learned about her."

CHAPTER 10

Susan hadn't really *found* Annie, per se, she'd found Betty Williams, a friend of Annie's, who had seen us with Harvey and gone up to Susan to ask where Dave was, which then somehow led into a conversation about Annie. I didn't hear all of Susan's convoluted explanation of how the conversation had come around to the third woman in Dave's life, but it was something that had involved fall foliage, then Benzes, then who was the cuter *ER* doc.

"What did Betty finally tell you?" I asked. "About Annie, not the probability of George Clooney returning to the cast."

"That Annie lives in Cleveland, which really isn't all that much of a drive from here and—" at this, Susan drew in a breath "—that she has five kids."

Kids.

The word slapped me, dropped into my gut with a sense of unfairness, of loss. That was supposed to be *our* next step, a baby to fill that empty bedroom at the top of the stairs. As I had for fifteen years, I'd put it off, figuring there'd be time. Time for me to get over my parenthood phobia, time for Dave and me to talk, for me to tell him the truth about how I felt about the baby issue.

Time, it seemed, had had the last laugh. "Dave had children?"

"Well, Betty didn't say that exactly. She just said Annie had five kids." Susan's gaze softened and I wondered if she had been struck cold hearing that word, too. "That could mean anything, Penny."

Five seconds ago, I had been planning on grabbing Susan and hopping in the Benz, heading back to Newton without stopping for hitchhikers, blown tires, emergency births or anything else. But the new information opened a window in me, a window that was both painful—

And curious.

Despite how my heart constricted like a rubber band had been tied across it, I wanted to know more. "Did she say if Annie was his wife?"

Susan's attention dipped into her purse as she looked for a tube of red lipstick and a little mirror. "I think we need to go see her," Susan said, avoiding the question as she smeared the tube across her lips, turning them from faintly pink to shocking crimson.

Something lurked beneath the surface of that L'Oréal, I was sure of it. But Susan had already replaced the tube and turned guileless eyes on me. "Shall we get Harvey registered for the show?"

"I left him with Matt, his doggy agent. I've done my part."

Susan reached out and took my arm, her grasp firm. "You don't honestly mean to leave Dave's dog here, do you?"

"That was my plan."

"Since when?" Susan put her other fist on her hip. "I thought we were down here to get to know Dave through Harvey. And his people."

"I've done enough of that," I said, lying through my teeth.

"Uh-huh. We know almost nothing more than when we started out. There has to be something else."

My nonchecked list already told me that. I rubbed at my neck, trying to ease the building tension. "On top of that, Matt wants *me* to take Harvey trotting around the ring for the show. He says Vinny gets stage fright and Harvey will only work with certain people and—"

"That's a wonderful idea!" Susan exclaimed, now pumping my arm up and down, using my extremities to emphasize her point. Two women passing by with We Love The Smokies shopping bags stopped and stared. Behind them, a slower-moving group of seniors was making its way down the sidewalk.

"It's a terrible idea. For one, I have no training in this and for another—" Well, I couldn't think of another just now, but I would.

"You should do it, Penny. It'll help you stop being so—" She cut herself off and bit that perfect red lip.

"So what?"

"Well…" Susan paused, her gaze darting away, then back as if this was such a scandalous thing to say she had to make sure the entire busload of seniors with their red Merry Manor Retirement Home sweatshirts didn't overhear. "You are a little *uptight*."

"I am not."

Susan just arched a brow. Apparently taking a fifteen-hour car trip with me had made her an expert on my personality.

"Why don't *you* march Harvey around?" I asked her.

"Because that dog won't listen to me. Why do you think I gave him to you?"

Thinking back, I realized Susan had hardly interacted with Harvey the whole time we'd been together. It was as if she were afraid of the dog, or maybe vice versa. If anything, I was sure the heels put him off. Little dog like that, tall spiky things near his paws…it had to look bad from his perspective. "I can't, Susan. And I won't."

"Not even for Dave?"

"Why the hell should I do anything for Dave?" The Merry Manor crowd turned around, making no secret of their staring. I lowered my voice and whispered the words again.

"Because you used to love him, just like me, and he would have wanted Harvey to strut his stuff."

"Dave is—" I still couldn't speak the word, not without it choking up my throat "—gone, and he wouldn't know if Harvey strutted or not."

"Yeah, but you'd know and you'd feel bad."

Susan was presuming an awful lot.

"I can't talk about this now. I can't decide right now." I ran a hand through my hair, trying to make sense of the thousands of thoughts going through my head. I needed some time to regroup. Get my bearings.

"Listen, why don't we stay here tonight?" Susan smiled. "Everything always looks better in the morning."

For once, I couldn't argue with Susan. After the

long day, the exhausting drive through the night, I wanted nothing more than a good night's sleep and a bit of distance between all of this and me. "All right. Just one night. Then we either go to Cleveland or back home."

Susan hesitated only a second before nodding. Second thoughts or simply her not paying attention? "Right. And while we're here, you'll think about letting your hair down a little?"

"I think I already did that."

Susan snorted a little in disbelief. "I know your personality, Penny. I see it in my lawyer and the man who does my taxes and that career counselor who tried so damned hard to convince me that I could be a flight attendant. I mean, could you see me in one of those ugly uniforms, handing out peanuts?"

Actually, I could, but I kept that to myself.

"You have everything in your life so tightly controlled, that one step outside the gate has you worried that the whole ball of wax will come crashing down. I mean, you have *wet wipes* in your glove compartment for eating *French fries*."

Susan made it sound like a felony. "I don't like the Benz to get dirty."

"You stopped me from putting salt on my fries, in

case the salt sprayed. It's salt, Penny, not mud." She shook her head, then went on. "You can live danger-ously and everything will be as it was in the morning."

"How can you say that after the week we just went through?" I turned away from her, willing the stupid tears that kept springing to my eyes to take a perma-nent vacation. "Nothing will ever be the same again."

"That's what's so wonderful," Susan said, pumping my arm again, like an oil rig that had hit a big cache of crude. "We can change. Do something different. Try a new life."

"I don't *want* to try a new life. I liked mine just the way it was."

Confusion knit Susan's brows together. "Then why did you marry Dave? I mean, he was all about change. About doing something different every day."

And then I knew. I knew what had gone wrong; I knew why my husband had needed another wife, another life.

Because I represented sameness. Ironing on Tues-days, scrambled eggs on Sunday. Sex on Wednesdays and Fridays, a kiss goodbye in the morning, a hug hello at night. Lasagna on Sunday—

God, I had been a walking, talking stuck record. Who the heck wanted that when they could have a shiny new iPod, one that came with bigger breasts and better shoes?

What made me think that returning to my old way of living wouldn't net me the same result? Assuming, that was, that I moved on someday, considered another relationship.

What if I did, and ended up in the same boat as before? With a man so tired of the ennui that he had to seek something else to fill his days?

I looked down at my button-down silky shirt and gray trousers, all as neatly pressed as they had been the day they'd come out of the dry cleaners. Lines aligned, buttons were snapped, lint hadn't dared tread anywhere near me.

"You're right, Susan." If there'd been a list of top ten sentences I never expected to hear come out of my mouth, that was number one.

She beamed. "Of course I am. So, will you do it?"

"There's really not much to it."

I wheeled around and saw Matt standing there. How long had he been there, listening? And what was he thinking about me and my wet-wipe issues?

"You walk Harvey around a ring," Matt said, coming closer, "and toss him a treat from time to time. He'll do all the heavy lifting."

I looked down at the tiny, wriggling ball of fur at my feet and thought I'd done nothing but heavy lifting since Dave had died. If the piano-playing dog wanted to take a few of the concrete blocks off my shoulders, I'd buy him a year's supply of Beggin' Strips.

CHAPTER 11

Georgia was thrilled when I called her later that night from our hotel room, a space that had all the personality of a cardboard box and about the same decor. "I knew this was going to go well for you, Penny. I had a feeling about it."

"Going well?" I thought of the flat tire, the hitchhikers, the E.R. run and then Matt's idea that I trot Harvey around. I'd left him with a dog, and without a commitment, because as much as I worried that my status quo was half the problem in my marriage, it still represented comfort. Organization was my life afghan and right now, I needed that crutch. "That's like saying the *Titanic* had a great maiden voyage."

Georgia laughed. "Look at it as an adventure."

I glanced toward the closed bathroom door of the La Quinta Inn room Susan and I had rented. The Grand Resort Hotel had been full and we'd opted to share a space. I'd proposed it as a money-saving idea, since neither of us knew how the estate would pan out. Truth be told, she was beginning to grow on me.

And, the thought of being by myself didn't exactly make me jump for joy. The last thing I needed late at night was to be alone with all these thoughts about why, and how, and when and where. I'd done altogether enough of that already.

"It has been different," I told Georgia. "That's for sure."

"Different is good right now, Pen. I know you don't think so, but it is."

I murmured something noncommittal. Different had never been my strong suit. I didn't plan on adding it to my personal deck of cards anytime soon.

"Oh, and you need to give Dave's mom a call. She left a message on my machine, looking for you. Said something about wanting to clear up something unusual in Dave's estate."

I sank back against the bed, balancing the phone against my shoulder, and pressed my hands to my temples. "Do you think she knows?"

"She's his mother. Don't you think she would?"

"I was his wife. And I had no idea."

"Oh, Pen, you'll figure it out." A doorbell sounded

on Georgia's end. "I'm sorry, hon, but I gotta go. My shiatsu massager is here."

"You have a massage therapist who comes to your house?"

"Oh no, not a person. A machine. Without you around to keep me busy, I've gotten hooked on QVC." Georgia laughed. "So either send me money or come home soon."

"I'll be home soon as I can. There are a lot of…loose ends."

Georgia paused and I could almost hear her sending me a mental hug. "I hope you find what you're looking for, Penny."

I glanced at the bathroom door, where Susan was inside, singing a Beatles song as she showered. "To be honest, I'm not quite sure what I'm looking for. Or what I've found."

I told Georgia I loved her, then hung up and lay back against the pillows. A plan, that's what I needed. I pulled out the pad of paper from the hotel, then started making a list of everything I wanted to cover tomorrow. Questions I still had, goals I hadn't hit.

1. Find out who Annie is
2. Decide what to do with the dog

3. Call Georgia; ask her to take another look
   in Dave's study for a will
4. Meet with Vinny. Tell him no way on the
   dog show idea
5. Determine legalities of this mess
6. Get myself untangled from the same mess

With each numbered item, calmness descended over my shoulders. Order was being restored, at least on this particular slip of paper. I studied the program guide for the Dog-Gone-Good Show, then tossed it to the side and slid under the covers.

The calmness ebbed, replaced by a wash of grief so strong it would have knocked me over if I'd been upright. The loss crushed my heart, squeezing it like an overjuiced orange.

Inside the bathroom, I heard the hair dryer start. The noisy Conair muffled my tears. I clutched the list, as if holding it could give me back the security I'd lost.

It didn't. All I got was a paper cut.

A few minutes later, Susan left the bathroom, clad in a silky blue nightshirt that skimmed her thighs. Quite the contrast to the oversize T-shirt I'd gotten for opening a Christmas Club account. I tried not to think about whether Dave had seen—and appreciated—that nightshirt and the slim, busty woman beneath it.

"Penny?" Susan asked after I had turned out the light. In the dark, her voice sounded miles instead of just a few feet away in the other double.

"Yeah?"

"Why do you think Dave did it?"

"I don't know," I answered, rolling over and clutching the second pillow to my chest and trying to get comfortable on the cheap mattress, avoiding the dip in the center. I could make out Susan's slim shape beneath the blankets, her back to me, her hair in a loose ponytail.

"I always thought I was the one, you know what I mean?"

"Yeah." What woman suspected her husband had an extra wife on the side? It certainly wasn't something you saw on Maple Street in Anytown, USA. Maybe there were bigamists on every street corner, but I doubted it.

"It's like that guy on *Oprah*, did you see that show?" She didn't wait for my answer. "He had nine wives. *Nine*. And they all lived in, like, the same state, and they all thought he was this big-shot navy pilot or something. I don't know how he kept that many secret. At least you and I live in different states." Susan was quiet for a long moment, and the dark seemed to wrap around us, joining us in a way that we hadn't been before. "Do you think Dave was like that?"

"With nine wives? God, I hope not."

Susan paused a moment. I could hear the alarm clock flip the numbers from 10:56 to 10:57 p.m. "What did he tell you he did for work?" she asked.

Susan was trying to do what I had set out to do— uncover what was lies and what was truth. But I didn't want her questioning my husband. To me, he was mine, always had been.

Susan had come *after* me, after Dave had said "I do" and "I promise" to *me*. Annie, if she even was a wife, had come after that. I was the first, I had the owner-ship claim.

But what did I really own? A man who'd run around the country, slipping marquise-cuts on women's fingers, while taking his piano-playing dog on the road?

Not exactly a big prize at the bottom of my box of Cracker Jack.

"What did he tell you?" I asked Susan.

"That he worked in insurance. That's how we met, you know."

Oh God. I didn't want to hear this story. I didn't

want to know he had met Susan at one of the office parties I had skipped because it had been tax season. Or that she'd been the receptionist at the office, there to greet my husband every day with a smile and a stack of pink messages.

But Susan apparently lacked the ESP gene because she went on, undeterred. "I was in a car accident, a hit-and-run on the highway, when I was coming back from visiting a friend in Boston. This guy switched lanes and nicked me, sending my car into the guardrail. I was standing there, on the side of the highway, crying. I didn't know what to do. I'd never been in an accident before and I was clueless. But then, Dave saw me and pulled over, got out of his car, and he helped me figure out what to do. Who to call, all of that."

"That's Dave," I admitted. It was the husband I had known, a man who would stop and help a little old lady who had dropped her groceries, who never passed a man broken down on the side of the road with a hissing radiator without running to the closest gas station to buy him some water and antifreeze.

"And we got to talking, and because I was still so upset and shaky, he offered to drive me home. And we stopped for coffee and—"

"One thing led to another," I cut in, not wanting the

sordid details. Not wanting to picture them, swept up in the moment and hurrying off to the nearest Motel 6.

"No, not at all. It was a long time before anything like that happened. We kept in touch because I was having problems getting my insurance company to cover the accident and all, so he was kind of like my adviser."

A friend. He'd started as her friend.

It was the exact way we had come together.

"So how did you two meet?" Susan asked, the question sounding like the kind you asked at a class reunion or a cocktail party, not in the darkened hotel room you were sharing with your husband's other wife.

Nevertheless, she'd told me her story, and in that guilt women seemed to inherit along with breasts, I felt compelled to do the same. "I met Dave in college. He was a business major, I was going for finance, but we had a couple of classes that overlapped the two majors so we ended up in a study group together. We were friends, really, nothing else. Then he came up to me after a business ethics class one day, and asked me out. I said no."

"You did?"

I nodded. "But he didn't give up. He asked me out again the next day, but I still wouldn't agree."

"Why?"

"He wasn't my type. I like men who are studious

and quiet." I laughed a little at the memory, the image I'd had for my future back then. "I guess I pictured myself marrying a professor in a tweed jacket. You know, the kind with the patches on the elbows? We'd sit in the study, him smoking his pipe while I balanced the checkbook or read the *Wall Street Journal*. We'd pour a glass of brandy and talk about world politics."

Susan let out a yawn. "Oh, sorry. That wasn't for you. It's been a long day."

I almost yawned myself at the thought of the future I'd once wanted, thinking it would have been so safe, devoid of the hairpin turns my younger years had held. "Dave didn't fit that image."

"He is the complete opposite of the tweed-and-pipe-smoking kind of guy."

"Not to mention, every professor's worst nightmare," I said, laughing again, the memories seeming sweet in the dark, not painful. "Dave was the class clown. He'd crack up the class at the worst possible time."

"He *was* good with a one-liner, wasn't he?" Susan's voice was soft, tinted with grief.

In that shared thought, a bond began to develop between me and Susan. Not the one forced upon us, but one that was growing out of the natural event of loss, and of sharing Dave.

"Yeah, he was." I said. "He even… Oh, I shouldn't tell you."

"No, go ahead. I'm fine. I want to hear about what he was like. It's almost like being with him."

Susan was a stronger woman than I. There was no way I could have lain here, listening to her top ten favorite memories of my husband and found it anything short of torturous. But she seemed genuinely interested and the urge to voice Dave's name had grown stronger in me, as if saying these words would help make all that had happened seem real, not some distant dream had by another woman.

"At our wedding," I said, my mind winging back fifteen years as easily as if it were two hours ago, "when the pastor got to the part about whether there were any objections, Dave said—"

"Wait, I know this. Let me ask my lawyer for a second opinion," Susan finished. "And then, he looked around, asked some poor guy who barely knew Dave if he had any objections, which about gave the pastor a coronary until Dave grinned. Five seconds later, the whole chapel was laughing and making lawyer jokes."

Something hot and sharp stung at the back of my eyes. "He said that at your wedding, too?"

"Yeah, but Penny, you know Dave. Once he had a good joke, he used it everywhere he could."

"Yeah." I drew in a breath and rolled over, clutching a pillow to my chest that would never take the form of the husband I had lost.

In the space of a few minutes, I had lost more than a husband. Every memory I had of him was now tainted. I'd never be able to sit in his favorite chair again, flipping through our photo albums and thinking I was the only one who had heard that line, felt that kiss on my cheek, known that event.

He'd doubled everything, damn him, and now he'd stolen more than my life. He'd taken my memories, too. "I'm tired. I'm going to sleep."

"Okay," Susan said, but her voice said she didn't believe me. I thought of apologizing to her for being short and crabby, of trying to explain, but I couldn't. She meant well—if there was one thing I'd learned about Susan and her nonstop chatter, it was that she meant well by every word—and I wasn't in the mood to hurt anyone else today.

Silence descended over the room, heavy and thick as a vat of peanut butter. I lay there, pretending I was asleep but really staring into the dark, busy hating my husband.

I hated him, I hated the dog, I hated the entire

situation. I didn't want to get to Annie's house and hear Dave's best lines again.

To hell with Cleveland. Let Susan rent a car and go meet Annie. Susan seemed remarkably well-adjusted to this whole thing, as if it were just a step out of her ordinary day. She'd been chipper and bright, as happy-go-lucky as a leprechaun. While I had a perpetual my-husband-betrayed-me stew cooking in my intestines.

Georgia had said I could do this, that it would be good for me to take a walk outside the perfectionist ring.

Fear tightened its grip on me. No way. I wasn't strong enough for this.

Then the fleeting thought that this dog show could actually be fun ran through my mind. How would being a part of this change the Penny Reynolds I knew?

I shut the thought off, shoved it to the back. I'd already had one major life change this week. I'd hit my quota.

Tomorrow, I was going home and going back to work. To something more normal than a dog show and the *Groundhog Day* version of my marriage. A few days of tax preparation and I'd be deep in columns and rows, straight lines and balanced totals.

And maybe, just maybe, with enough little green grids, I could fool myself into thinking that I'd never heard Susan regurgitate what had been one of my fondest memories.

Yeah, and maybe the book of tax code updates from the IRS would be a little light reading. I wasn't simply looking for a miracle.

I was looking for a rearrangement of the cosmos.

CHAPTER 12

It was Harvey who convinced me to stay.

Matt showed up early the next morning, undoubtedly clued in on our location by Susan, who seemed determined to keep me here.

And who seemed equally determined to sleep till noon. I couldn't rouse her, no matter how hard I tried or how many times I opened the blinds and lifted her eye mask. She just groaned, rolled over and went back to snoring.

"Guess it's just you and me," Matt said. Harvey, who'd been waiting patiently at Matt's feet, let out a yip and raised himself onto his back paws. "Oh, and Harvey."

I refused Matt's offer of breakfast and led him down to the quiet lobby, figuring the best thing to do was tell him I was leaving. Before he got any ideas that involved me, a stage and a dog who played the piano.

I sank into one of the crushed red velvet chairs, while

Matt chose the one opposite. Harvey came over, plopped himself at my feet and then looked up, expectant. "I don't have a Milk-Bone, if that's what you're after."

"He's not," Matt said. "He's concerned."

"He's a dog. All he cares about is eating, sleeping and dropping a surprise on the neighbor's lawn."

Matt chuckled. "Harvey's got a lot more than that in his emotional repertoire. He's empathetic, too. He knows you're upset and he's worried."

I rolled my eyes. A dog that was worried about me. Yeah, right.

"I think he missed you, too. Last night, he paced my hotel room and whined half the night."

"He misses Dave. Harvey and I didn't meet until two days ago."

Matt sat back in surprise. "You're kidding me. Dave had a dog and you didn't know?"

"Dave also had a second wife and I didn't know."

Matt nodded. "True."

I reached into my purse, pulled out my list and a pen. Best to start right at the top. "What do you know about Annie?"

Matt shifted in his seat, moving from the relaxed, ankle-over-the-knee position to two feet on the floor and his back against the seat. "Not much."

He was lying. Why? To protect me? To protect her? "Is she another of Dave's wives?"

A couple with a bichon frise walked past us, chattering about the upcoming show and how well their pooch would do. "Blue ribbon," the woman said, confident and sure. "Isn't that right, Hemingway?" She nuzzled down and kissed the dog, her face disappearing in a mess of fur.

"I never met Annie," Matt said after the couple was out of earshot.

"That doesn't answer my question."

"Listen," he said, leaning forward, elbows on his knees. "I think you've been through enough. You don't need to add to that pile."

"What I need is to find out what my husband was keeping from me," I said. "Besides the dog."

"Oh, it's Harvey!" An older woman, somewhere in her sixties or seventies, came hurrying over to us, bending at the knees to greet the dog. Harvey looked to me, as if waiting for permission to greet a member of his fan club. I shrugged and Harvey moved forward, ears perked, back straight. The woman looked up at me. "Can you make him do his *Swan Lake* thing? I so love the way he dances. He reminds me of my Fred. God rest his soul."

"Uh, Harvey is a little tuckered out right now," I said, considering I had no idea what Harvey's *Swan Lake* routine was, or how to make him do it.

She pouted. "I really like that dance."

"Maybe later."

The woman harrumphed and gave me a glare. "Dave always did it for me. Where is he, anyway?"

I swallowed. "He passed away."

"Oh, Lord, I'm so sorry." The woman pressed a hand to her chest, her face filled with the embarrassed flush of trying to extract a foot from her mouth. "Please give his family my condolences."

"I will." All three of them, I added silently.

The woman bent to give Harvey a quick snout kiss before leaving. She hadn't gone more than five feet before she stopped another woman and passed on the news about Dave.

I sighed, turning back to Matt. "I didn't think it would be this hard to tell people."

Matt leaned forward and placed a hand on mine. "I'm sorry that you're going through all this."

"Yeah, me, too." His palm on the back of mine was comforting, warm. It seemed a million years since anyone had touched me. I shook off the thought, then straightened. "Tell me everything about Annie."

Matt let out a gust and leaned back into his seat. "Penny, let it go."

"Why? What are you not telling me?"

"Meeting Annie isn't going to help you get over losing Dave."

I ignored what he said. It *would* help me. It had to. I didn't have any alternative plans. I had Susan and Annie and an unfinished puzzle with my husband at the center. I swallowed hard, closed my eyes, then forced out the one question I had yet to voice. "Are there any others?"

"No." But what hung in the air after his answer was the unspoken *not that I know of.*

None of this told me why. Why Dave had needed another woman or two, why I hadn't been enough. "Am I the kind of person you'd picture with Dave?"

It was Matt's turn to swallow, to shift again in his seat, then he took a good, long look at me. "You're a confident woman. Strong. Organized as hell, I can tell, just by that list. All numbered, prioritized and laid out in perfect rows and columns. I bet you're one of those people whose hall rug fringe is all in alignment."

I chafed at the description. Being organized wasn't a sin and was, indeed, the one thing my husband had said over and over again that he appreciated about me.

Or had he?

"In other words, I'm not the kind of woman Dave would go for."

He considered that for a moment. "More the kind of woman Dave needed."

"What's that supposed to mean?"

"You're the kind of woman who likes things to add up, to have everything in your life fit on little labeled shelves."

"I don't label my shelves," I said, bristling. Okay, so maybe I had labeled the ones in the linen closet, but that didn't count. I was merely following Martha Stewart's example. "I plead the Fifth on all the rest."

Matt sat back and grinned, a good-natured smile that didn't condemn me for my Type A personality. "Dave was…spontaneous and quick, but a total slob. I know because I roomed with him for a week once in Denver." I wanted to ask what year, what day, and compare that with my calendar, but I didn't. I'd had enough illusions shattered already. "He was a guy whose idea of order was pulling up to a drive-through window." Matt's green eyes softened and he leaned forward, his face earnest. "He needed you, Penny, to keep him on track. To keep him sane. If he went looking for something more, then he was a fool, because he already had everything he needed right here with you."

Tears welled up in my eyes. For God's sake, the last thing I wanted to do was start crying in the lobby of a La Quinta Inn.

Nevertheless, the tears spilled from my eyes, trailed down my cheeks, plopped onto my jeans, spreading in dark denim puddles. "I'm sorry. I hate to cry."

At the last word, Harvey took off at a scramble, darted over to a nearby table and yanked a tissue out of the box, nearly toppling it in the process. He came skidding back, then dropped it gently in my hands, the thin paper barely dented from his tiny teeth.

I blinked, looked at the dog, then at Matt. "Did you just see that?"

He grinned, as if Harvey hadn't done anything more exciting than sit up and beg for table scraps. "I told you, he's empathetic."

"He…he knew I was crying?"

"Harvey knows a lot more than you give him credit for."

I glanced again at the Jack Russell terrier, sure this time that I did see sympathy in his wide, wise eyes. Tentative and slow, I reached out a hand and stroked the dog's head. Soft, almost silky fur met my palm, not the wiry fur I'd expected. He scooted an inch, maybe two, closer, then pressed his head to my knee and let out a puppy-size sigh.

"How can you leave a face like that?" Matt said, grinning again.

Oh, damn. I couldn't.

It was as if Dave himself were sitting there, looking up at me. The damned dog even had the same eye color as my late husband.

I let out a breath and, with it, the weight that had been sitting on my chest all night.

Whether I liked it or not, I needed this dog, and he needed me. We'd both lost Dave. I swiped my eyes, blew my nose, then gave up the idea of returning anytime soon to my happy place of organized cabinets and straight lines.

"Okay," I said, to both Harvey and Matt. "What do you need me to do?"

CHAPTER 13

An hour later, it became clear that walking Harvey around the ring of the Dog-Gone-Good Show involved a lot more than just watching while Harvey did his thing, tossing him the occasional bit of kibble for his efforts. The whole thing was definitely a huge dog-and-pony show—

With me as the pony.

Apparently, a different routine was needed to impress the judges who had already seen Harvey in action. Matt promised Vinny would help me develop a new rotation of tricks before the next morning. "Harvey's a little rusty," he said, "and you're new at this, so it might take you some time."

"How much time?"

"You have eighteen hours until the show. I'd say that's about enough." Matt took my hand after we had returned to the Grand Resort Convention Center, where I was supposed to meet Vinny, and gave me a smile. "You'll do fine, Penny. I have no worries."

"I do. This kind of thing is *so* not my forte." Harvey sat at my feet, patient and seemingly way more confident than I felt. "You don't know me very well."

"No, I don't." His gaze met mine, something unreadable in those emerald-colored depths. "Yet."

Then he walked away, leaving me with another monkey wrench in my plan to get in, get out and not get involved. And yet, also with an odd surge of confidence that maybe this wouldn't be as bad as I thought.

I'd always wanted to be capable of spontaneity, of that kind of relaxed, easy fun I saw other people having. Maybe this was my big shot at the normalcy I'd never really achieved.

I tried calling Susan from the lobby phone. No answer. Either she was at the nearest Payless Shoes or sleeping the sleep of Dracula.

"Yo."

I turned around and saw a large man striding toward me, eating a burger as he walked, even though it was only eight o'clock in the morning and a loaded Big Mac wasn't exactly a portable food.

He was short and squat and had a swinging,

penguin walk that seemed to tip him precariously from side to side. He wore a T-shirt emblazoned with a huge red heart around the head of a terrier, faded jeans and worn, scuffed cowboy boots.

"Are you Vinny?"

He popped the last bite of burger into his mouth, seemed to swallow it as is, then threw out his arms with a flourish. "The one and only. Trainer extraordinaire. Isn't that right, Harvey boy?" Harvey took the opportunity to leap upward, right as Vinny brought his arms together and caught the little dog, hauling him to his chest. "How's my boy? You bein' good? You eatin' right? You's a good boy, aren't you?" Vinny snuggled his face into the dog's fur.

It was an odd juxtaposition, the fat man cuddling the tiny dog, but it seemed to work, at least in this alternate universe I'd inhabited ever since Dave's wake.

"He being good?" Vinny asked me, chuckling as Harvey made good use of his tongue against Vinny's vast, bouncing cheek.

"He's fine. A little…skittish in the car."

Vinny roared with laughter. "Pissed on your seats, did he?"

I nodded.

"Dave should have told you. Harvey gets a little

nervous in the car. Best off keeping him in his crate."

"It wouldn't fit in the Benz."

Vinny roared again, making his belly jiggle like Jell-O on speed. "Harvey pissed in a Benz? That's better than when he did it in the cab Letterman sent for us. Damn, he ticked that cabby off. The guy was cursing at us in two languages." Vinny reached out and put a hand on my arm. "I have one thing to tell you. Plastic."

"Plastic?"

"Yep. Hermetically seal your seats and Harvey can't do much more than create a puddle. A few sheets of Bounty and wham, you're on your way again."

I thought of Dave's car, the twin to mine, sitting in the garage. Someone had brought it home—the cops, his brother, I had no idea. Both sets of seats were coated in plastic, the kind you bought at the hardware store for paint jobs. A memory came back, clear as the sun, slamming into my chest.

"You know how I spill, Pen," Dave had told me, smoothing the plastic over the leather, tucking it into the creases.

That had been three, no, four summers ago. Dave in the driveway, me outside with him, holding his glass of iced tea and watching him work. He'd put the plastic on, then asked me to help him wash the car.

I'd had enough of being outdoors and tried to back out of it, telling him I had stacks of files I'd brought home from work, waiting in the house for me to work on, but Dave had convinced me, with a sponge thrust to my chest and that irresistible dare in his eyes.

I'd grabbed the hose in retaliation, chased him around the car, both of us ending up in a wet soapy mess, and then, before I knew it, we were running into the house, up the stairs to the bedroom, where we'd spent the afternoon making love. The soap had dried on the car, leaving a white film over the paint, but Dave hadn't cared.

Nothing had ever seemed to stress Dave, to worry him. I'd been the one to worry double, to cover for his "it'll all work out" attitude. That afternoon, though, it had been like when we first met. Fun and spontaneous, completely out of my control.

Then the fax line had rung, work streaming in through the printer, and I'd slipped out of bed, even as Dave tried to convince me to stay, to chuck the responsibility for a day.

I shook my head, pushing the thoughts aside, along

with the pained hitch in my heart. Would it be so bad to throw aside the old Penny, just for a day? To try on something new, in the anonymous safety of strangers?

"So, tell me what I'm supposed to do with this dog." I forced a smile to my face.

Vinny chuckled. "It's not what you do with the dog, it's what the dog will do with you. First thing is to get him to listen." Vinny put Harvey down on the floor, and instantly the terrier snapped to attention. He sat at Vinny's feet, waiting patiently, his tail doing a soft swish-swish against the carpet.

"How did you get him to do that?" I asked. "Calm right down?"

"I'm the alpha dog," he said. Vinny, I noticed, had straightened his posture. All of a sudden he went from being a schlumpy wannabe biker to someone who commanded attention, at least from the canine set. "Dogs," he explained, "have a pack mentality. They need someone to be the leader. If you give off the air of being in charge, the dog will naturally respect you and wait for your cue."

"What happens if there's no alpha dog?"

Vinny chuckled. "Harvey runs roughshod over you."

"That I've seen. I think I'm the beta dog. Or whatever the lowest dog on the totem pole is."

"Not to worry. You can change that." Vinny crossed the room, shut the doors of the small ballroom, blocking any prying eyes. Harvey didn't budge from his spot on the floor. When Vinny returned, he glanced down at the dog, still patiently waiting for his command. "One thing you have to remember with dogs is to communicate. Dogs can't read minds, so if you're not communicating, he won't know what to do. Okay. Let's see what this boy can do." He slung a backpack I hadn't noticed off his shoulders, then withdrew three vinyl dog toys: a banana, a squeaky cat and an orange bone. He marked out several paces, then jumbled the toys into a rainbow-hued pile before returning to the dog. "Harvey, you ready?"

Harvey's swish-swish increased in tempo and his ears perked.

"Go get the banana."

As if he'd been zapped with a cattle prod, Harvey lunged forward, dashed across the room and went straight for the pile of toys. He nosed the top two out of the way, picked up the yellow faux fruit, then turned and trotted back, his prize proudly between his jaws. He held it until Vinny put down his hand to exchange the prize for a piece of kibble.

"How did he know which one was the banana?"

"Scent discrimination," Vinny said, the multiple syllable word slipping from his tongue as easily as Harvey had retrieved the banana. Apparently work mode brought out a different side of the trainer, too.

"Scent what?"

"All tricks start with basic obedience. Harvey first learns to fetch."

"Like your ordinary cocker spaniel?"

"Exactly. Then we take it up a notch. Start by putting out only the banana and telling him to get the banana. A few times of that and he associates the word with the toy."

"How does the scent thing work then? Is the banana scented?"

Vinny laughed. "Not like a fruit. Like a hot dog." He reached in the backpack and pulled out a baggie holding a wiener marked "Banana."

"You rubbed hot dog on it?"

"If you were a dog, which toy would you grab? The one that smelled like a Barbie doll or the one with hot dog cologne?"

"I'd go for the one with Chanel No.5 myself."

Vinny laughed. "Good one." He reached again into his bag, withdrew a beach ball and blew it up, then handed it to me. "You want to try a trick with him?"

I shook my head. "But I'm not alpha dog."

"Just pretend you are," Vinny said. "The dog will believe you."

Could I do that? Pretend my way into the top dog spot? I glanced at my left hand, at the wedding ring that I had yet to take off. Wasn't that what I'd been doing all along, all my life really? Pretending everything was just fine?

I straightened my spine and gave Harvey a stern glance, one I'd seen often enough in my childhood to have it memorized. Harvey sat down and stilled, waiting for me. Wow. Maybe there was something to this Alpha Dog thing. "Okay, what do I do now?"

"Put that ball on the floor in front of him, then back up to the wall."

I did as Vinny suggested, walking backward, keeping my eye on the dog. Except for the occasional glance at Vinny, he maintained his sentry position. "Now what?"

"Tell him to play s-o-c-c-e-r."

I gave Vinny a dubious glance but went along with it. "Harvey, play soccer."

Harvey leaped to his feet, bent his head down and pressed his nose to the ball. Working one step at a time, he nosed it to the left, then the right, following a straight path across the carpet, right up to my feet and then through my legs.

I stood there, stunned. Harvey had done it. *I'd* done it.

"Score!" Vinny shouted. "Now, give him a treat."

Just as quickly, my elation deflated. "A treat? Uh, I don't have any. I left his little bag of Beggin' Strips in the car."

"First rule of dog training," Vinny said, crossing the room and dumping a few dog-food pebbles into my palm, "is to keep some kibble in your pocket. Always reward him."

I put all but one of the treats into my jeans. Eww. Now my clothes would have that special eau de Purina. Try explaining that to the dry cleaner. Beneath me, Harvey danced around the ball, waiting for me to put out my hand. When I did, he snarfled up the single treat, leaving a streak of saliva across my skin.

My wet wipes never seemed so far away.

"He needs some practice," Vinny said, "but I think he'll do fine tomorrow. Still, I think his mood is a little off."

To me, the terrier seemed his usual peppy self. Then again, what did I know about canine moods?

"Must be losing Dave," Vinny said, bending down to tickle Harvey behind the ears. The dog submitted to his touch, then rolled onto his back, offering up his belly. "You miss him, don't you, guy? Yeah, me, too."

"Me, too," I said, so softly I almost didn't hear the words. An odd mixture of regret and anger settled in my stomach. As much as I missed him, and the life we'd had together, another part of me would have gladly shoved that banana down Dave's throat.

"What do you know about Annie?" I asked, reminded that as much fun as it had been to play Pelé to Harvey, there was an extra-wife reality waiting to be dealt with. I had to pose the question sometime and thus far, no one seemed to know anything—or rather didn't want to tell me anything. I hadn't felt this sheltered from the truth since I'd been five. "Have you met her?"

"Nope. Never met any of Dave's—" Vinny wisely cut off the sentence. "Uh, anyone else in Dave's life, except for Matt, of course."

"Then why did you call me Annie? And how did you know he married her?"

Vinny heaved a sigh and rose, leaving a disappointed Harvey on the gold-and-red carpet. "I don't want to speak ill of Dave. He was a good guy. A real man's man."

"Meaning, he could juggle a few wives and still knock back a beer after he and Harvey ran through the dance program?"

Vinny didn't flinch at the anger in my tone. He just kept standing there, calm as a summer lake.

"Sorry," I said. "I've got a lot of issues with Dave right now and since he's not here to beat up, I'm taking it out on you."

"Understandable." Vinny gave me a short, quick nod. "I don't know much about Annie, just what Dave told me. And I kinda assumed they got married after Dave talked about it."

"What did Dave tell you?"

Vinny reached into his pocket for a dog treat and tossed it down to Harvey, watching the dog chew before he spoke again. "You sure you want to know?"

No, I wasn't sure. Regardless, I steeled myself for the worst and went back to pretending everything was just fine. "I have to. There's an estate involved."

Vinny waved a hand in dismissal. "Leave that shit to the lawyers."

I couldn't. I had to know, if only so that the next time I went home and curled up in the chair with that afghan, I wasn't sitting there in total blindness. Moving on wasn't an option, nor was thinking about myself, not until I'd cleared up the semi parked in front of my heart. "What do you know about her?" My voice cracked on the last word.

Vinny shuffled from foot to foot, the alpha gone from his stance. Clearly, he was one of those men who could handle a Doberman but not a woman who sounded like she was about to cry. "Mrs. Reynolds—"

"Penny, please. I already share that name with far too many people."

"Penny, then." He patted the front pocket of his shirt, then let out a curse. "Gave up smokes a month ago, but there are days…" His voice trailed off.

"What do you know about Annie?"

Vinny gave up on searching for an invisible cigarette and let out a curse. "Dave met her last year, at the UKC show in Ohio last February."

"UKC?"

"United Kennel Club. Harvey here is a mutt, so he can't participate in regular AKC stuff. Annie had a pointer mix she'd entered in the competition, his first time doing it. To see what he'd do, you know? Smart dog, but hyper as all hell. Dave, though, could get that thing to calm down. Dave had a way with dogs. Not just Harvey, but all dogs."

"Dave was the alpha," I said.

"Yeah, but in a gentle way. Like that Robert Redford guy in that movie with the horse. He was…" Vinny shook his head, chuckled a little at the memory of Dave. "He was good with dogs, but too soft to be a good trainer. He was always cuddling the damned dog instead of getting him to work."

I looked down at Harvey, trying to imagine my husband holding him close, the brown-and-white body against his favorite blue button-down shirt.

The image refused to appear. Instead, the only one I saw was Dave in the casket, the blue button-down shirt making its final appearance on his stocky frame.

"Anyway, after the show, I guess Dave took Annie aside, showed her some of the ways he'd learned to work with Harvey."

"You weren't there?"

"Harvey ain't my only client."

"Of course." I waited, my breath caught in my throat, wanting to hear what he said next.

And at the same time praying Vinny caught a sudden case of laryngitis.

"It worked out real well. Within a few hours, Dave had that dog fetching 'bout anything you told him to. He wasn't so good at the obstacle-course thing. Had this fear of the A-frame."

"And then? Where did it go from there? How did it go from dog tricks to a wedding ring?" My breath was lodged in my throat so tight, the anticipation of what I'd hear next knotting my stomach.

Vinny looked heavenward, as if wishing for a bolt of lightning to save him from an uncomfortable situation. "Dave was between gigs with Harvey, so he went out to Annie's place for a day or two, showing her how to work with Max."

I swallowed hard, the pieces clicking into place, the lies throwing off their robes like *Playboy* models.

My husband had been gone for eight days last spring. Straightening out a corporate insurance mess at some Cincinnati beauty products company. Or at least, that's what he'd told me.

I thought of those daily calls home. How short and brief our conversations had been, marked by the distance that had grown between us during that year. A wall, put up when he'd raised the subject of a baby. Again.

An idea I'd vetoed. Again.

I closed my eyes, what-ifs careening around my brain, silver balls in a pinball game that was already at full tilt.

"What else?" I asked, my voice nearly a whisper.

Vinny grimaced the pained look of a man who'd

rather be buying Kotex at the CVS. "There's not much else."

"What else?" The words gritted past my teeth.

Vinny drew in a breath, tossed another treat Harvey's way, then shifted his weight to the other foot. "Annie was in a bad spot financially. Something happened, and I swear, Penny, I don't know what, that made Dave rush on back there soon as he left her, telling me he was getting married. He even canceled a gig Harvey had in Denver."

Dave's words echoed in my head. "There's more to this than I thought, Pen," he'd said. "A couple more days and I'll be home."

"He never told me why he went back there or what all went on," Vinny said. "All I know is that he had Matt cut her a check."

A brick sat on my chest, adding to the ton already there. Before this was over, I'd be able to build a damned school. "How much money?"

Vinny shrugged. "Me and Dave, we didn't talk dollars. Just Harvey."

I closed my eyes, digested what I'd just heard, but it sat heavy in my stomach, like my Aunt Elsie's tuna casserole. "When was the last time you talked to Dave?"

Vinny thought back. "October? November? I don't

remember. The fall's pretty much a blur. I was, ah, getting treatment. For my little, ah, stage problem."

The information about Annie was still sinking in, slamming against my already bruised heart like strong surf waves. I wanted to go home. "Are you over that problem?" I asked with a hopeful smile. Matt could have been wrong. There might not be any reason for me to take Harvey through his plastic banana routine. Besides, all this talk of Annie had erased my temporary fog of confidence. "You know Harvey the best. Can't you do this show?"

"Are you kidding me?" Vinny's face paled a couple shades. "If you knew what that Rin Tin Tin replacement did, you wouldn't be asking me that question." Vinny eyed me squarely. "Let's just say he retrieved something that wasn't a banana."

I shook my head, confused, and glanced at the pile of rubber toys on the floor. "Did he grab the bone instead?"

"A bone…of sorts." Vinny waved a hand over his belt area. His eyes squinted up in the agony only a man could experience. Sweat broke out on his brow.

"Oh. Oh my God." I had to force myself not to look at Vinny's button fly. "Why would he do that?"

Vinny shook his head, the sweat multiplying. He swiped the back of his palm over his forehead. "Sometimes there are disadvantages to carrying dog food in your pocket."

I glanced down at my jeans and then at Harvey. Thank God I didn't have a banana hidden behind my fly.

"I can't talk about it anymore." Vinny threw up his hands, a red flush spreading from his temples to his throat, the beginning of hives raising on his skin. "I tried like hell in therapy but there are just some things a man shouldn't have to endure. And that's one of 'em."

"Well, Harvey would never do that." I gave Vinny a hopeful, work-with-me smile.

Vinny put up his hands, warding off the idea. "I can't do it! The minute I get out there, with all those damned lights and the clapping and the dogs…" He shuddered, the hives now becoming mini facial mountains. "Flash-back city. I think I got some of that post-trauma stuff."

Harvey got to his feet, prancing excitedly around us, clearly trying to get the two humans back to playing fetch.

"Post-traumatic stress syndrome? From Rin Tin Tin's replacement?"

He leaned forward, his eyes daring me to disagree. "You ever have a dog latch on to the wrong hot dog?"

"Uh…no."

"Until you've walked in my jeans, lady, don't try and get me up on that stage."

"But—"

"You can do this," Vinny said, grabbing my arm. "I've never been very good in front of people anyway. I only did it because Dave—"

He cut off the sentence as fast as he began it.

"Dave what?"

Vinny cursed again and shuffled his feet some more. "If Dave went on *Letterman*, people would know about it."

"Yeah? So?"

"People…like you."

"I see." I turned away, ignoring the hot sting of tears. It had all been an elaborate scheme to keep the Wife without a Clue in the dark. "He went to an awful lot of work to keep his secret, didn't he?"

"He was a good man, Penny. Would have given a homeless man the shirt off his back."

"Or a needy woman the ring in his pocket."

Vinny swallowed, silent.

"Bastard." The word spewed from me in a fast flash of anger. Harvey dropped to the floor, head on his paws, cowering against Vinny.

Oh damn. Once again, I'd lashed out at the wrong person, or in this case, the wrong mammal. Because Dave, damn him, had gone and died. Harvey watched me, his eyes wary. Remorse filled me. I dug in my pocket, then bent down and reached out to the dog. He hesitated a moment, then took the kibble. "Sorry, Harvey."

That was enough for the dog. He got to his feet again, rising onto his hind legs and doing a little doggie pirouette. I rewarded him, then let out a breath. This dog was made for performing. Lived for it, even.

Right or wrong, Dave had had a plan for this dog. And just because my husband had been a jerk in gentleman's clothing didn't mean I had to cut off the dog from what he loved, too.

Despite the circumstances, I *had* had fun. In the short time in the ballroom, I'd found something I hadn't had in a long time. A side of myself I thought disappeared years ago.

Maybe I could do this. Change the course of my life, not go off in a whole other direction, but maybe dip down a side road or two, and by doing that, eliminate what had led to this mess. "What does it mean if Harvey wins this show?"

"He does Dave proud." Vinny bent down again, stroking Harvey's head. The tension in the dog's shoulders eased. "Dave might have done a lot of things wrong, but he loved this dog."

"Yeah." I sighed. "It's too bad he didn't love me, too."

CHAPTER 14

I had thought that working with Vinny and Harvey would make me even more confident but, once away from the ballroom, I began to feel the complete opposite. By the time we finished learning the new routine, I felt about as sure of myself as I had in middle school, about to reveal my lack of breasts in the girls' locker room during gym.

Vinny had told me to try to be natural and loose. "Harvey can feel your stress. You gotta let it go. Breathe, baby, breathe."

Hyperventilating probably wasn't what he had in mind.

I strode through the lobby, narrowly avoiding a Chihuahua-schnauzer brawl, Harvey happily trotting along at my heels, pausing every now and then to glance up at me. Several people greeted Harvey, many calling him over to say hello, but the little dog stayed resolutely by my side, his quartet of legs moving at double speed to keep up with my stride.

I kind of liked having him with me. Harvey had become an odd comfort in this strange dog-show world.

The Grand Resort Hotel was overrun with dogs, their owners, and the continued craziness of the registration fray. Chatter ran at a high volume, coupled with excited squeals of long-lost friends meeting up and barks of dogs establishing territory. There were women dressed to match their dogs, men walking beside dogs that seemed nearly as tall as small trees, children darting in and out among the canine confusion.

"How'd it go?"

I stopped at the sound of Matt's voice, his deep baritone carrying a note above the barks, growls and whines. And that was just the noise of the owners.

Matt stood by the bank of lobby phones, the unstressed, casual opposite to me. He had changed into a soft blue sweater that set off his eyes and the dark brown of his hair. A powerful combination, if the stares of the women in the hotel lobby were any indication.

"It was…a learning experience," I said. One I hadn't exactly mastered.

Maybe I could, my mind whispered. After all, Georgia, Matt and Vinny all thought so. Three-to-one odds. Or maybe it was the opposite, considering I'd never gambled.

If I could somehow tap into that part of me they saw—the part that could master a dancing, singing, ball-playing dog routine—then maybe Harvey could put on a good show.

Either way, I refused to let a dog show get the better of me. Or worse, retreat into the same old Penny, who clearly had been lacking something.

"Vinny's quite the character, isn't he?"

"He gives Loony Tunes a whole new meaning."

Matt laughed. "If you promise not to run off, I'd like to offer you some dinner. We can get out of this craziness." He gestured toward the hectic lobby zoo.

"Susan—"

"Is with Jerry again. He's so smitten, he's even taking her to the mall."

I laughed, the sound still foreign enough that I wondered for a second if it had come from me. Heck, the whole thing was foreign—me trotting out jokes, engaging in what might even be considered repartee. "Dinner sounds good."

In fact, it sounded more than good. I hadn't had a full meal in days, my stomach too tied up by the stress to tolerate more than a couple of bites of anything.

Appetite roared to life in my stomach, not just for food, but for something resembling normalcy, or at least a step toward the normalcy other people had.

We fell into step together as we crossed the lobby. I glanced over at him. How long had it been since I'd gone out to dinner with a man? Months, at least. Dave had traveled so much that he never wanted to go out when he got home.

Was he taking the other women out, and thus, had nothing left when he finally returned to me?

I pushed those thoughts aside. It was dinner, with the dog's agent. Matt wasn't a boyfriend, or even a potential one. There was no reason to feel guilty, to second-guess a simple meal. Or to still feel as married as I'd felt last week, before I'd lost my husband.

Because in reality, I'd lost him a long time ago.

Instead of taking me to a restaurant, as I'd expected, Matt ordered a couple of sandwiches to go from Seaton's Café inside the hotel, then led me outside and around the back of the building. Beside us, the Little Pigeon River ambled along, tucked into lush greenery and tall, budding trees. The water skipped over rocks, making its way, as water always does, around the stone impediments. We strolled along the path, eating our sandwiches, soaking up the end-of-the-day warmth.

It was wonderful. I inhaled, breathing in the scents of nature, the freedom that seemed to carry along the air.

Harvey trotted along at our feet, content to sniff his new surroundings and nab the occasional bit of sandwich meat tossed his way. He looped in and out of us, stretching his leash, clearly excited about being outdoors. A squirrel darted up a tree and Harvey lunged for the rodent, natural dog instincts kicking into high gear. I tugged gently on the leash. "No squirrels, Harv. Not tonight."

He'd already started after a twig, clearly not upset about the no-hunting policy.

Matt and I paused by the stream, watching tiny fish weave their way around rocks. The water was the color of weakened tea, its quiet movement nearly as soothing as a good cup of chamomile. Harvey barked at one of the fish but danced away from the water's edge.

Suddenly, I didn't want to spoil the day, the easy mood between myself and Matt, with talk about Dave. "Tell me how Harvey came to be. Tell me everything." Then a smile slipped across my lips. "Leave out the bad parts."

Had I just made a joke? The woman who had the

deadpan abilities of a table? Matt's little chuckle verified that I did, indeed, have a sense of humor.

"You're a woman of contradictions," Matt said. "When I first met you, I never expected you to be funny."

"I'm not normally."

We'd finished our sandwiches and tossed the wrappings into a wastebasket along the path. "I find that hard to believe," Matt said, his gaze sweeping over me with an intensity I hadn't felt from a man in a long time.

"Oh, get to know me better and you'll see. I'm happier with an adding machine than a one-liner."

He laughed again. "See, like that."

"Tell me about Harvey," I said again, suddenly uncomfortable with the attentions of another man. "If I'm going to pull off this Milk-Bone circus tomorrow, I need all the ammunition I can get. And if there's some part of Harvey's psyche—assuming a dog that weighs about the same as a big stack of hardcovers has one—that could help, then I should know about it."

Vinny's words came back to me. If Harvey won, he'd make Dave proud. I shouldn't care about making my bigamist husband proud.

But I did. Because as much as I wanted to dump the blame for this entire mess squarely into Dave's coffin, a tiny part of me whispered that it took two to tango, and two to crumple a marriage.

Matt picked up a rock and skipped it across the water. It bounced twice, then sank. Harvey let out a yip of approval. "I met Dave seven years ago, at a convention."

"A dog convention?"

"No, an insurance one."

"You sold insurance?"

Matt chuckled. "Yeah, for about five minutes. I'm a lot better with canines than I am with death amortization tables." He shook his head. "Sorry. I don't normally stick my foot in my mouth this soon into a date." He paled a bit. "Not that this is a date, just—"

"It's okay. Really." And it was, I realized. The shock was starting to ease, a tail wag at a time. And to me, this wasn't a date, just an…information scavenger hunt, with the dog along for chaperone. Although, considering how distracted Harvey was by the environment, we could have run off to Vegas and the dog would have never noticed a thing.

What if it had been a real date, though? Would I have been interested in Matt? I slid a glance his way and immediately felt a surge of attraction in my gut.

I shook it off and got back to the dog. "Did he have Harvey then?"

"Yes and no." Matt smiled, waited while another couple strolled by us, their hands linked and their conversation the easy one of long-marrieds, then went on. "Harvey kind of showed up outside of Dave's motel room. Scared, hungry, thin as a pencil, and looking more like a rag doll than a dog."

"He didn't belong to anyone?"

"Not that Dave could find. He ran an ad in the paper, called the local vets. Pulled out all the stops to try to find Harvey's owner, but no one came forward." Harvey turned toward us, perked an ear up at the mention of his name, then went back to his vigorous sniffing campaign.

"What city were you in?"

He looked surprised at the question but answered it all the same. "Minneapolis. Why?"

"I'm trying to piece it together with what I know." I flipped through the mental files of my life and found that one, standing out as if it had been stuck in a red folder instead of manila, marked with *Turning Point* in big, bold letters. "It was 2000," I said. "I remember that conference."

"You were there?"

"No. Dave asked me to go. Mall of America had opened a few years earlier and he thought I'd like to go, to see it and shop. But I turned him down, probably because I had quarterly returns to prepare or something else that seemed more important at the time."

We both knew what that refusal had meant. It had been the start of Dave's turn away from our ordinary life. I couldn't play the what-if game, not now.

I needed to unravel more of these dangling threads. Maybe then, I could knit them back into something that made sense.

"What did he do with the dog?" I asked. "After the conference?"

Matt looked surprised that I wouldn't know. We started to walk again, Harvey happily in the lead. "He didn't bring him home? I guess I always assumed that's what Dave did."

I shook my head. "He asked me about getting a dog, around that same time. And I said…"

"No," Matt finished when I couldn't, when the word choked in my throat, realizing how many blocks I'd put up to my husband's dreams. "It's okay, Penny. Not everyone is a dog person and you have a right to say you didn't want a pet. People do it in America every day." He smiled, but I couldn't bring myself to echo the gesture. "You don't seriously think that because you said no when Dave suggested you two get a dog that you made him go out and find another wife?"

"Let's just say I didn't help the situation." I bit my lip and turned to look at the street outside the hotel, watching a multihued ribbon of traffic stop for a light. Matt laid his hand over mine, holding Harvey's leash, and me.

Matthew Shay was a man who touched people, who connected with them. No wonder he hadn't enjoyed the world of insurance, a business where you had to remember details and calculate the probability of someone dying, as well as the financial toll wreaked by someone's grandma getting hit by a bus.

"You didn't cause him to do that, Penny," Matt said softly. "Men leave their marriages all the time, some of them for very stupid reasons."

I didn't look at him until the light had turned green, the cars slipping through the intersection.

"Most of them don't go out and find the replacement before they've dumped the first one. And worse, hold on to a marriage that clearly wasn't working. At least on his end."

But how well had it been working on my end?

"You're a wonderful woman, Penny." Matt squeezed my hand. The touch of his palm was both comforting and oddly sensual. I hadn't been touched by another man in fifteen years, and a quick blast of guilt cooled the sensation. Dave was gone, but he was still alive in my heart, despite everything.

"I've known Dave for years," Matt said, "and I'm sure the last thing he wanted to do was hurt you."

"Well, he did." If I bit my lip any harder, I'd never need lipstick again.

"Hey, don't cry," Matt said, still holding my hand. "You'll scare the fish."

"I think Harvey already did that." I turned to look at him and felt a smile curve across my face. "Thank you."

"For what?"

"For taking my mind off of things. For reminding me that I'm not some evil harpy who drove my husband to cheat. For reminding me…" My voice trailed off.

"What?"

I swallowed, watching the way the breeze toyed lightly with Matt's hair. "For reminding me I've got more qualities than just my ability to create a spreadsheet."

This time, he laughed. "Anytime. I'd be glad to list your qualities. Just not on a spreadsheet." He shook his head, feigning horror. "That brings back bad insurance nightmares."

Despite the tears threatening at my eyes, I laughed. I caught his gaze. Something serious and heavy hovered in those deep green eyes. I slipped my hand out from under his, pretending to be suddenly interested in Harvey's foraging for food along the grassy edge.

"Do you want to change the subject?" He cleared his throat, as if he'd sensed it, too. "Away from Harvey and all that?"

I plucked a green leaf off a low-hanging branch and shredded it, watching the pieces flutter to the ground, confetti for my path. "No, I want to know it all. Actually, that's technically a lie. I don't *want* to know it, I *need* to know it. There's an estate and money and—"

"And a heart that needs closure?"

I had to blink several times before I could speak. "Practicing psychology in your spare time?"

"No. I just know how it feels to be betrayed. All you want to do is figure out why."

"So I can avoid repeating history later."

"Yeah." Matt fell silent for a moment and I wanted to ask him about what had happened to him, about what was now clouding his eyes, but I didn't.

My own problems were a big enough mountain. Besides, I wasn't here to get to know the dog's agent or to start something with the man—regardless of that flicker of attraction I'd felt—I was here to master a dog show and get some answers. Maybe later…

There'd be time for a man like Matt.

"So, did Harvey do tricks when Dave found him?" I said. "Or did Dave teach him that later?"

"Harvey came with a few. The tissue thing? He did that. He could jump over things, and through a Hula-Hoop. And, he'd retrieve about anything you asked him to. He has quite the understanding of words. But the counting, the singing—"

"He sings?" Harvey turned toward me, a twig in his mouth, as proud of himself as the first caveman to discover fire.

"Uh-huh. Better than me." Matt grinned again, traces of the earlier emotion gone. "All that, Dave and Vinny taught him, over the years. Harvey took to it, like the proverbial duck."

"How did you come into the picture?"

"Well, I didn't stay in insurance for very long. I'm not the kind of guy who likes being stuck in an office all day, filling out paperwork. By the end of the convention, I knew insurance wasn't the field for me. All those men in one room, getting excited about policy riders and risk management." Matt mocked a yawn.

I laughed. "They are like that, aren't they? Trust me, accountants are exactly the same."

"So that's the secret to you then. Throw out a few tax returns and next thing I know, you're doing the limbo?"

"Not exactly. But I do like when things add up."

"And what happens when something doesn't?"

"I keep gnawing away at it until it does."

"This, you know, might never add up. Not entirely."

"Yeah, I know." I looked out over the water and drew in a breath. "It's got the people factor, the one thing that doesn't fit nicely into Excel."

"You'll figure it out, Penny," he said, the confidence in his tone inspiring a little in me, too.

I didn't want to like him, to be attracted to him, but I was. He was the first man in years who had seen something in me other than my ability to calculate numbers.

"Thanks," I said, and meant it. "Anyway, I interrupted your story."

He nodded, sensing my shift back to business. "When I got back home to New York, I had lunch with a friend of mine who's a book agent. I was looking for a job like that, where you weren't stuck in a cubicle and every day represented something new. Books didn't excite me, but it got me to thinking about Harvey, about the possibilities with the dog. So I hooked up with Dave again."

The sun was nearly gone, leaving little flecks of gold reflecting off the water. We pivoted to turn back, both unconsciously picking up the pace a little. The temperature had dropped and I wished suddenly that I had brought along a jacket.

Nevertheless, for my first dinner out with a man in a long time, it had been fun—if I discounted the conversation subject. Matt was an enjoyable person to be around, and someone who had made hot sandwiches and a meandering walk seem like a five-star restaurant.

And, he'd done something else I hadn't expected or sought—made me feel wanted. Like a woman, not just a wife or an employee or a dog owner. A real, honest-to-goodness woman who attracted him.

That was heady stuff, and I put it on the back-burner for now.

"Why did Dave hire you as Harvey's agent? You had no experience." How could Dave have hired someone who had opted for this career on what amounted to a whim? If it had been me, I would have put Matt through the job interview from hell, complete with personality tests and a fully vetted résumé.

Dave had operated on feelings, I operated on facts.

Yeah, and look where that had gotten me. Completely oblivious to the facts of my life.

Matt shrugged, a boyish grin on his face. "Dave thought I could be something, so he gave me a shot. We hunted up a trainer and before you knew it, Harvey was in business. In the beginning, he was doing bit things here and there, appearances at nursing homes, a few commercials and a couple times he doubled for dogs on other shows. Then he was in a movie and that was his first big national break."

"Did Dave make good money at this?"

Matt nodded. "After a while. It took time to build up Harvey's name and reputation. But once Dave made it his full-time job, the dog's career took off."

I stumbled. *"Full-time job?"*

Regret washed over Matt's features. Clearly, he realized he'd let slip another detail, that again, I didn't know. How many secrets was I going to uncover? How far would this go before I could finally feel I knew what I needed to know, to go back to my life? Or would it keep unfolding for years, a continued pile of Band-Aids stacked one on another, trying to mask a massive betrayal?

"But, I thought he still worked at Reliable Insurance. I saw his car there all the time."

"He, ah, kept an office in the same building as the insurance company where he used to work," Matt said.

"So I wouldn't put it together."

"Yeah."

"Wow." The sandwich I'd eaten earlier now sat like a heavy rock in my stomach. "Guess that cements my status as Clueless Wife of the Year. I had no idea, because he still got together with those guys. I went to the office Christmas party with Dave last year, for God's sake."

"Dave was the kind of guy who kept his friends. You know how he was. Everybody liked him."

"Especially the women."

A wry grin crossed Matt's face. "I didn't know about the other wife, Penny. I really didn't."

"He never mentioned he was married?"

"Oh, he did. When I first met him. He talked about you."

Me. Maybe there had been a time when, for Dave, I had been enough. That he had been happy in our marriage, that I hadn't imagined all of those days out of some desperate attempt to hold on to a fictional world. "What did he say?" I wanted to slap myself for grasping at that straw.

"He loved you, Penny, that I could tell." Matt cleared his throat, the male part of him seeming uncomfortable with this whole discussion of emotions, particularly those in another man's heart. "I don't think he intended for it to become what it did. Remember, he kept it all from me, too. It wasn't just you. I never met Susan or this Annie you asked about. I only heard about you."

"But you heard *something* about Annie. I know you did. I saw it in your face when I asked you in the lobby. And you wrote her a check. What for?"

Matt's attention went to the road, as if watching the cars zooming by would provide some clue to how he was supposed to proceed. "With Annie, you're going to have to meet her yourself. I don't know—and that's the truth—what her relationship with Dave was, but there was something there, I'll acknowledge that. Dave only mentioned her once, when he needed that check expedited to her address. I didn't ask questions. I was Harvey's agent, not Dave's counselor."

He was telling the truth, of that I had no doubt. I thought of my list, sitting squarely in the front pocket of my purse. I hadn't crossed off a single thing yet. Every question I asked seemed to lead to even more of the same.

I left it in my purse. The list could wait.

I nodded. "Thank you for being honest."

"I don't know much else," he said, his tone apologetic, as if he wished he could just hand me everything Dave had kept to himself and be done with it. "I don't know where Harvey stayed in between performances, either. I never asked, because Dave seemed to have it all under control. All I did was set up the gigs, process the contracts and the money."

The money. The practical side of me sprang to life. The last thing I needed in probate court was another surprise. "How much money?"

We paused at the last juncture of the path, Harvey panting a bit with all the excitement of his outdoor adventure. "Last year, Harvey made just under a half a million dollars."

I nearly choked instead of inhaling. "One dog can make that much?"

"He keeps pretty busy. Does movie work, commercials and print ads. You probably saw him in that dog food one?"

I shook my head. "I had no idea Dave made that much."

"He didn't keep it all. He made donations to shelters all over the country. I guess he didn't want to see any other dogs end up on the streets like Harvey had."

A bittersweet smile crossed my face. "That's Dave. The bleeding heart with his wallet open."

Matt ran a hand through his hair, displacing the dark brown waves. "I don't know if you've thought about the future or not, but Harvey does have a pretty full schedule ahead of him. I haven't canceled or confirmed anything. I didn't know what you'd want to do."

I remembered the tour outlined in Dave's notebook. Six cities, starting in June. An *Oprah* appearance just before that. I was okay with doing the dog show, as some sort of karma payback for whatever side of the marriage fault line was mine, but after that, I was done. And in a weird way, I wanted to prove I could do it. That I could be something other than a wife so boring, my husband had started up an extra-curricular life.

"I can't throw my life aside to go travel the country with a dog, Matt. I'm only here for this one event, to get Harvey through the Dog-Gone-Good Show. While I'm here, I wanted to find out what else my husband was doing behind my back."

"I'm not asking you to take Dave's place. I understand this is hard for you. I just want you to think about it for a couple days. Maybe, if you want, you can designate someone else to be Harvey's guardian, and then the show can go on, so to speak."

Give Harvey to someone else. Let another person

tour the country with the dog, taking all ringside performances off my shoulders. It was the solution I'd been seeking, yet a part of me resisted the idea.

What was I thinking? That Harvey and I would become the canine and human equivalent of Barnum & Bailey? I shook off the thought.

"That's a great idea, Matt. Can you find someone else?"

A flicker of what looked like disappointment ran through his eyes. "Sure. I'll get on it first thing." Then he led the way up the path back to the hotel's convention center.

Thinking about giving Harvey up hit me with an odd sensation, as if I was packing off a piece of myself. A piece I'd just discovered, between the trip down here and the conversations with Matt.

So much for my life spreadsheet.

CHAPTER 15

I headed down the makeshift hall that led to the performance area for the Dog-Gone-Good Show, Harvey at my heels, his little body a tightly wound spring of anticipation. I stood there, waiting while the A/V people attached a mike and battery pack to my jacket, and wondered if it was too late to back out.

I'd called Georgia an hour before, panicky and ready to run. "You'll be fine, Penny. Think of it as giving the valedictorian speech back in high school."

"Only using a dog instead of three-by-five cards?"

Georgia laughed. "Yeah."

My high-school delivery had been made to humans, not canines. And I hadn't been expected to make my speech, then roll over and play dead. "I don't know, Georgia. This is more your kind of thing than mine."

"How do you know? You've never really done anything that took you out of your bubble."

"I took a road trip with my husband's second wife. I'm holding a dog who can play soccer."

"And I bet you also have a list in your back pocket, with a whole schedule planned out for Harvey's day in the sun."

"It's in my sleeve, for your information, not my pocket. Besides, I have to have an outline. He has this complicated routine and—"

Georgia sighed. "Penny, let go of the lists. Let go of the pier, jump in the water."

"What is that supposed to mean?"

"Live a little on the edge, or maybe let Harvey take the lead and see where that gets you. It won't kill you to do something totally improvised, you know."

"I've done that before. It didn't work out so well."

"One mistake doesn't have to turn you into Control Cathy." Georgia sighed. "I love you, Penny, but you're about as spontaneous as a pickle."

It was time to go. I'd said goodbye to Georgia and a few minutes later, found myself herded down the temporary hall, then left to wait among the Airedales and shelties. Nervous canine and human energy filled the space.

I could do this. And I wasn't the only one who

thought so. I sucked in some confidence, then straightened. And prayed.

The program started, the announcer brought out the first competitor, and a shushed quiet fell over the group, broken only by the outside sounds of the announcer and the occasional burst of applause from the audience. Beside me, one man prayed, another woman popped one Tic Tac after another as if they were candy and a second woman incessantly rubbed the furry fuchsia hair of a troll doll between two fingers.

And then, along came Cee-Cee.

The poufy poodle and her pushover owner crowded into the waiting area, taking up more than their fair share of space. "It'll be okay, Cee-Cee," her owner soothed. The poodle danced in place, whining and shaking, which made her pink tutu shimmy, like a dog stripper. "Shh, shh, baby."

That only served to wind Cee-Cee up more. The dog wheeled around, straining against its leash, poking its pointy manicured nails into everyone within stepping distance. I scooped Harvey off the floor, yanking him out of hyper pink-bowed puffball range.

Vinny had given me a mini tuxedo for Harvey to wear, which made him slippery in my arms. I'd thought the dog would resist, but he submitted to the little suit jacket and tie, obviously familiar with costuming. Harvey wriggled against me, nearly as worked up as the other dogs. Clearly, he sensed what was about to happen and was looking forward to it.

At least one of us was filled with anticipation instead of the overwhelming need to flee. I tamped it down. Doing this, I knew, would be good for me. Might even be…liberating.

After all, hadn't I married Dave, seeking to find that side of myself? Then I'd gone and stuffed it in the cedar hope chest with my wedding dress.

"And now, Harvey the Wonder Dog!" the announcer called, with all the drama of Rod Roddy.

Tension double-knotted my stomach, tempered with a flush of excitement. It was too late to back out now. I glanced over my shoulder and saw Vinny standing against the wall, red faced and breathing heavily. Pink lotion dotted the eruptions on his face. He flashed me a wavery smile that spelled clear relief he wasn't the one going out among the dogs and people.

I could do this, I repeated in my head, over and over again. Then I moved forward, Harvey trotting along, right in step with me. A couple of Vinny's helpers had set up Harvey's course in the few minutes between dog acts. I glanced around, seeking a friendly face.

Third row up sat Susan, next to Jerry. She sent me a little wave, Jerry gave me a thumbs-up. Behind them, Matt simply nodded, a confident smile on his face. For some reason, that simple gesture inspired an internal burst of can-do spirit.

I made a simple, quick hand movement that Vinny had taught me when we had run through Harvey's routine yesterday, working in the ballroom in two separate sessions, to give Harvey a breather in between.

Harvey saw the signal and took a seat at my feet. "Harvey, are you ready?" The mike on my lapel broadcast the statement to the audience. I put my hands up and out, Harvey's response cue.

He shook his head no. The audience roared with laughter.

"Don't you want to work?" Hands up and out again. Harvey repeated the no.

"Do you want to play instead?" This time, I moved one of my hands up and down, just a flicker of movement, but Harvey's attentive eyes saw it. He responded with an emphatic nod. Now the crowd was really laughing.

Wow. This was actually working. I, Penny Reynolds, Accountant of the Year two years running, was standing in a ring with a dog and putting on a show. I conjured up my inner Julia Roberts and moved on.

"Too bad, Harvey," I went on, "because we have work to do. Are you ready?"

I made the movement again, but timed it to delay the response a moment, as if he were thinking about it. He gave a yes again, eliciting more laughter and applause as Harvey got to his feet and came along with me.

We reached the first station set up for his routine. I picked up the first prop, a copy of Walt Whitman poems, something that seemed apropos of Dave and all his years of self-exploration.

Harvey stood at my feet, waiting for his cue. "You're all dressed up. Do you have a party to go to?"

At my signal, he did his yes.

"Then it's time for a little training in the social graces. Get ready." He plopped his bottom on the carpet, then waited while I balanced the book on his head. "Show me your good posture." A quick flick of my index finger upward, and Harvey carefully raised his little body up, balancing on his hind legs, keeping the book in place. The audience clapped and whistled.

Who knew I could become Greta Garbo with a Jack Russell terrier as my co-star? Every time he listened to me, and did what he was supposed to, I was stunned.

I slipped Harvey a piece of kibble, then moved on to the next stop, painfully aware of the hundreds of eyes watching us. No wonder Vinny got stage fright. Between the heavy, silent anticipation and the pressure of so many spectators, it was enough to give *me* hives.

A lump of nerves formed in my throat. I swallowed, but that only moved the lump to my gut. I refused to feel the nerves. I could do this. And I would. "Okay, Harv, here we go," I whispered to him, then stood to address the audience. "Great job with your social graces. But I hear that Chihuahua you like over there—" I pointed in the direction of a dog waiting in the wings for her turn to go, adding a flourish to my movements "—wants more than a date. She needs a *hero*."

With a dramatic whoosh, I yanked a red cape off a small chair, then held it in front of me. "Let's see how you are in the defensive arts. Time to bullfight."

At the last word, Harvey backed up, scraping his rear paws against the carpet, à la the fiercest bull in Pamplona. He lowered his head nearly to the carpet, swinging it left, then right. He scraped his paws again, let out a snort, then charged forward, running through the red fabric, just as I jerked it away.

The crowd hooted and clapped. Laughter rang from the walls.

I smiled, elation soaring inside me. This was the Penny I'd always wanted to be—a woman confident in her own skin. In that moment, I knew a part of me had been changed forever—

And in a damned good way this time.

Harvey spun, retook his bull position and repeated the trick. When I gave him his treat, I noticed a gleam in his eye. The dog was eating this up.

We moved on to the banana trick, then to his obstacle course. He clambered up the A-Frame, across a skinny beam, down a set of steps and then across a zigzagged board in record time, stopping at the end to pounce on a springboard that sent a ball up a pole. It bounced against a bell at the top, ringing like a carnival game.

He caught his dog-food reward midair, leading me nearly as much as I was leading him. His eyes were bright with excitement, clearly in his groove. I felt that way, too, more than I ever had in the office.

We headed to the musical station, where one of Vinny's helpers pressed the button on a CD player, sending music through the room.

"If you want to impress the girls, Harvey, you need to learn how to dance. How about a cha-cha?"

Harvey rose on his hind legs and spun around,

dancing on his back feet, pawing at the air with his front feet. He dropped down as the chorus began and raised his little snout, releasing his own soulful version. I sneaked a peek at my card outlining his routine, then returned my attention to the dog. "Great job, Harvey." I tossed him another nibble, then flicked my finger to get him to move to the next trick.

He didn't move even though the CD had ended. Instead, he started singing again after eating his dog snack. I tried it again, hoping he'd get the hint.

Nothing but a badly warbled "Star-Spangled Banner."

"Harvey, let's play along," I told him, the verbal cue that was supposed to get him to move on to the toy piano.

Harvey kept up his singing.

"Harvey, let's play along," I repeated. Nervous tension twisted my intestines. It had been going so well. What was going wrong?

Harvey dropped down, looking at me expectantly. I gestured toward the toy piano. "Play along, Harvey."

He leaped up onto his hind legs and did the spin again, pawing at air, letting out little yips as he did.

Oh, hell. It was all going wrong now. I slipped my note card all the way out of my sleeve, then realized the notes for this trick were on the back. Curse me and my wordiness. I flipped it over. "Piano—Play Mozart," I'd written.

I'd given him the wrong command. I glanced over at the trio of judges, their faces set in frowns, all traces of humor long gone. Apparently Harvey's singing was only amusing for the first twenty seconds.

"Harvey," I said, mentally praying that he would pay attention, get a clue, rescue this situation, "playing along doesn't mean playing to the crowd, you big ham."

He lowered his head between his paws, doing *contrite* better than the best Oscar winner.

I'd been talking to the dog, forgetting that my comments would be broadcast to the audience. Their eruption of laughter told me they saw this snafu as a joke. Even the judges stifled a grin. Harvey's cutup reputation had saved us. And, so had my own spontaneity. Who knew I had a spontaneous side at all? "Harvey, show that little Chihuahua how you can *play Mozart*."

He let out a bark, then hurried over to the piano, plunking out a tune with his tiny nose. On the sidelines, Vinny's helper added a concert CD for accompaniment. With his tux and serious nose playing, Harvey was a hit.

When he finished, I gave him two treats, for saving our butts, then signaled for the next trick. "Time for you to get some rest, Harv. That way, you'll be fresh for your date tonight. Let's *take a nap*." He raced forward to a tiny bedroom scene, pulled the dresser drawer open, yanked out a dog-bone-decorated nightshirt and delivered it to me. I slid the shirt over his tuxedo, then sent him off to climb into the tiny bed.

"Get some shut-eye," I told him.

He leaned over and turned off the push-button nightstand light with his paw, then feigned sleep. The audience hooted with laughter and I saw a twitch of what could have been a smile on Harvey's face. With every trick, Harvey's enjoyment had increased exponentially with the audience's response.

He was a ham, but an adorable one.

For me, it felt as if I had hit my stride, if that was even possible in a situation so outside my normal frame of reference. I'd found a balance between being prepared and having to improvise. In an odd way, it was liberating.

Even fun.

Harvey's entertaining spirit had become a part of me. As scary as it was to change, even a little, I drew it in, and shot the dog a smile.

Harvey reached the end of his new routine, where he was supposed to engage in a gunfight with me. It was the part that had me most worried, not because I thought I might do any harm to the dog with the unloaded toy pistol, but because it was so new to Harvey, he'd stumbled a bit in practice with Vinny.

I slipped a cowboy hat onto his head, telling him quietly to keep it on. The dog glowered at me from under the brim, hating the head appendage. Vinny had warned me, but I hoped Harvey would at least cooperate for a short skit.

"Oh-oh, Harvey. Seems that Chihuahua has another suitor." I gestured again toward the miniature dog, now flanked by a poodle. "What are you going to do to be her hero?"

The last word keyed Harvey to retrieve a small wooden box from the table, drag it over to me, then sit down and let out a woof. I picked it up, opened the lid, then lowered it to Harvey's level. "Choose your weapon."

He fished one out with his mouth, then sat back again, a little woof escaping past the plastic handle. The audience chuckled. I bit back my own laughter. The dog that had seemed to be my nemesis had started to grow on me.

I pulled the second one out and put the box to the side. "Gunfight at the OK Corral? Are you sure?" I did the finger flick again and he nodded his head, even more emphatically than before.

The people surrounding us cheered and clapped. I couldn't have been more proud if it had been Georgia sitting there on her haunches.

"Okay, a duel it is." I spun around, waited until Harvey had backed his little body up against my heels. "Five paces," I said.

I marked off five steps, slow and easy, hoping like heck that Harvey was doing the same behind me. "Draw!" I said, in my best Clint Eastwood, before spinning around and aiming at Harvey.

He'd spun around and had his head tilted so the gun in his mouth was aimed in my direction. I waited for the popping sound, another technical detail added by Vinny's helper, but heard instead only two long, drawn out syllables of disaster.

"Cee-Cee!"

The poodle had broken free from her owner and was racing through the room, careening off the spectators, the obstacles. I glanced over at Vinny's helper, hoping the guy would tackle the overzealous poodle, but he was busy fumbling with the CD player, unaware of the pandemonium heading toward us. Just as he depressed the player's button, Harvey spun toward Cee-

Cee, cocked his head. The boom of a gunshot exploded from the sound system.

Cee-Cee, startled by the sound, skidded to a stop.

"Down!" I said to Cee-Cee, low and even, affecting as much alpha male as one widowed woman could muster.

The poodle wavered, then slid her front paws forward and lowered her white puffball frame to the ground. Harvey trotted over, and then, in typical Harvey drama, put one paw on Cee-Cee's back, as if he'd just nabbed himself a hell of a big white bear.

Applause boomed from the crowd as Cee-Cee's red-faced owner marched over, attached a rhinestone studded leash to her matching pink collar, then dragged her recalcitrant pooch offstage.

We'd done it. I looked down at the dog, stunned the routine had all come together and even better, been capped off by Cee-Cee's wayward entry. Pride swelled in my heart, for the dog, for me and even, yes, for Dave. I had no doubt my husband was watching and laughing.

For the first time since I'd stood before that casket, my grief began to ease, opening a window into a new existence.

"Take a bow, Harvey," I said, waving toward the crowd. Keeping his hindquarters up, Harvey put his front paws on the floor, then touched his nose to the carpet. Then he rose, pressed his body next to mine and did the same thing.

Something hitched in my throat. Harvey was a true star, all the wonder dog he'd been made out to be—

And yet, he didn't mind sharing the limelight, with me, the one person who hadn't wanted him around.

He'd captured the hearts of every single person in the room. And now, finally, he had mine, too. I'd never expected to like, much less love, the dog.

I flicked off the portable microphone attached to my pants, then leaned down and ruffled Harvey's head. "You did a good job, boy. And thank you for giving Cee-Cee exactly what she deserved. You and me, boy, we make a good team." I blew on my finger like it was a gun. At my feet, Harvey let out a woof of agreement.

CHAPTER 16

The applause for Harvey's performance and first-place finish, as well as winner of Best Dog Overall, thundered through the room, echoing off the convention center's walls. A Miniature Pinscher in the corner began to tremble, the noise clearly too much for his pixie-size ears.

Harvey looked up from his position beside my shoes, his brown eyes wide and intent on my face, expectant. I bent over, gave him a quick stroke on the head, then stood again, holding his trophy and blue ribbon tight. "Good boy. Good job."

Harvey kept staring, his tail still, his body rigid. I repeated my praise. Still, that tiny face remained fixed on mine, waiting for something. What, I had no idea.

I praised him again, the soaring feeling of completing something I'd never thought I could do still rising within me.

"Hey, Harvey! Good job!" Matt came up and joined

me as Harvey and I exited the ballroom, making room for the other award winners to take the stage for Best in Show, Best Costume and Best Attitude.

Cee-Cee's owner stood to the side, glaring at me. Clearly she blamed Cee-Cee's traumatic ordeal in the ring on Harvey. The poodle had been so shaken up by the bogus shooting, she'd thrown up on her owner's feet.

I couldn't say I blamed the dog.

"Vinny watched on the closed-captioned TV in the other room," Susan said, coming up to join us. She was still trailed by the infatuated Jerry, though Susan hadn't done much more than glance in the poor guy's direction. "He said Harvey did his best performance ever and to tell you congrats. After the crowd dies down, I think Vinny will stop breathing into a paper bag and come out and tell you himself."

"It was phenomenal," Matt agreed, a bemused smile on his face. "I had no idea you were such an actress."

I felt my face flush at his praise. "Oh, no, I'm—"

"It's a compliment, Penny. Don't bounce it back like we're volleying for serve." He bent down, ruffled Harvey's head, then stood again. "You both were amazing."

Still, I fidgeted. When was the last time I'd been complimented on anything besides the accuracy of my numbers? The odd feeling of pride that had blossomed on the stage now bloomed in my chest.

"Dave would have loved this," I said softly, tenderness curling around my memories of my husband. Dave would have been the first out with the "atta boys" and the call for a celebration. I looked at the glistening trophy, a golden dog sitting atop an A-frame obstacle, and for the first time since my life had been turned inside out, I wished my husband were still here.

My focus went to Harvey. He still stood at my feet, ignoring all the praise and pats on the head. He simply watched me, silent and unreadable. I reached into my pocket, found a lone dog treat and held out my palm for him to take it.

He ignored the treat and instead turned away, his attention going over his shoulder, sweeping the ballroom. His ears perked up for a second, then drooped. He let out a sigh and hung his head.

"I think he's sad," Susan said.

"He's a dog, he doesn't get sad." And yet, I wondered if maybe he was. In the past two days, I'd grown closer to that dog than I'd ever thought possible. Melancholy seemed to be hanging on his little shoulders. Maybe it was post-show letdown or some such thing.

The winners were announced a final time as the show wrapped up. Someone in the audience shouted a "Yeah, Harvey!" The dog's ears stood at attention again and he pranced in a circle, scanning the audience. But after a moment, his head sank again onto his chest. He dropped down and crumpled onto the floor.

"Do you think he's looking for Dave?" Susan asked.

"He's probably confused," I said, though what I knew about dogs would fit in a matchbook. "Every time he's performed here, Dave has been here to greet him at the end of the show. Maybe he's expecting Dave to show up."

I knew how he felt. Every step of this journey, I'd kept feeling Dave would be just around the corner, laughing at the prank he'd pulled. I'd see him walk into the room, his familiar smile and confident stride hitting me like it used to years ago, when I'd fallen so hard for him I'd committed the second biggest spontaneous act of my life—

Eloping.

Harvey, I knew, missed Dave. Harvey hadn't been at the funeral or the wake. He'd never seen Dave again after being dropped at Susan's house. He had no idea what had happened.

Oh damn. How did you tell a dog that his owner was dead?

"Let me get him out of this mess," I said to Matt and Susan. "I'll meet you guys out front. Maybe he needs to go out or something." I wove my way through the crowd, trying to reach the exit of the convention hall.

"Excuse me! What are you doing with Dave Reynolds's dog?"

I spun around at the sound of a woman's voice behind me. Tall and thin, her long brown, straight hair was a near match for that of the Irish setter at her feet. Before I could answer her, she was striding up to me. "Where's Dave? He never misses one of Harvey's shows."

"He passed away," I said, the words getting a little easier each time I said them, but still feeling like barbed wire as they left my throat.

She put a hand over her chest. "Oh, my! I thought I heard LouAnn Rawlins say that, but I didn't believe her. That woman is nothing but a gossip. Still, what a shock. He was such a great guy. We all loved him and Harvey. He's been a fixture here for years." The woman arched a brow. "But why are you working with the dog? Are you one of Vinny's helpers?"

"No. I'm Dave's widow." Or rather, the president of the Dave Reynolds Widow Club, but I kept that to myself.

"Oh, dear, I'm so sorry." The hand to the chest

again. "What an awful tragedy. He was so young. What happened?"

"Heart attack." The woman launched into another round of sympathetic sounds. I slipped on my polite face, the one I'd learned to perfect when teachers had asked me how things were at home or I made up some story for the guidance counselor about why our mother hadn't attended the meeting about Georgia's shaky grades.

"Were you a friend of Dave's?" I asked her.

"Oh, everyone was. He was one of the nicest guys I ever met."

I gave Harvey a little pat, but he didn't respond with more than a flicker of his tail. "Yes, Dave was quite charming," I replied, still polite.

"Well, at least you put one rumor to rest. People have been wondering about you."

"Rumor?"

The woman waved a dismissive hand. "Oh, some people have been speculating that Dave finally sold Harvey."

I looked down at the dog, who was still just sitting beside me, silent and as enthusiastic as a sock. "Sell him? Why would Dave do that?"

The woman shrugged, watching as her dog tried to initiate the canine waltz of sniffing. Harvey ignored him. "It was just something he kicked around once, a couple months ago at one of the other shows. He seemed real determined to do it. Even asked a couple of us if we were interested in taking on the Harvey franchise. But none of us thought he was serious. Dave loved that dog."

"Was he having troubles with Harvey?"

"Oh no. Those two got along like butter and toast. I got the feeling there was something..." Her voice trailed off and an uncomfortable stiffness filled her features.

"It's okay," I said. "Dave died so suddenly that I was left with a lot of unanswered questions. If there's something you can tell me to fill in the blanks, I'd appreciate it."

The woman took my arm and drew me over to one of the long seats that lined the exterior walls of the hotel. Her dog lay at her feet and let out a yawn. Harvey kept looking behind him, watching the people come out of the room.

"I got the feeling," the woman said, "and I could be totally wrong about this, but it seemed Dave wanted to change his life somehow. Like he wasn't happy with what was going on. It was the first time I ever saw him stressed. He said he was buying a new house and I don't know, maybe that meant some kind of change that he wanted to be ready for?" A weak grin crossed the woman's face, as if she'd just realized she might have told me too much. "Or maybe he was afraid Harvey would chew up the woodwork."

We had bought the house December fifteenth. I'd meant to get the Christmas decorations up that weekend, something I'd skipped doing for far too many years because I'd been too busy. Then a client called me on Saturday morning, needing help to clean up an end-of-the-year accounting mess. When I finally came home from work that weekend night, Dave had been there, a complete surprise, because he'd left the day before for what was supposed to be a three-day trip.

The tree was decorated, Bing Crosby was crooning "White Christmas" on the stereo, a fire was lit in the fireplace, candles were burning around the room, even my favorite cinnamon potpourri was simmering in a pan on the stove. He'd done it all, creating the one thing he knew would melt my heart because I'd never had one as a child—a traditional, homey Christmas.

He'd told me over a glass of wine by the fireplace, one of the coziest moments we'd had in months, that he was going to cut back on his travel because he really wanted us to make a stab at having a family.

Softened by the tender gesture of the Christmas tree and the melody of "Silent Night" in the background, I'd finally agreed.

"Was this around the middle of December?" I asked the woman.

She thought a bit. "Yeah. December seventeenth, actually. I remember because of Her Highland Warrior here." She gestured toward the dog with an embarrassed grin. "What can I say? I'm a romance novel fan. Anyway, my dog took his first ribbon in agility. Harvey, of course, was the favorite for first place in overall talent, but Dave had left before the competition on Sunday morning. We figured it was all a phase and he'd be back. We all expected to see him here." The woman looked over at me, at the ring on my finger and my grip on the dog's leash, then laid a hand over mine. "I really am sorry. Did you guys have any children?"

I shook my head. "No."

But it had been in the plans. I'd finally relented, thinking that maybe that was what I needed to do to keep my husband home at night, that if I had a baby, with Dave at my side, I'd get over my resistance to being a parent.

I'd also thought a baby might restore the spark that

seemed to have gone out between us, maybe even restore the zing that had deserted me, compounded by a husband who had grown more distant each year, physically and emotionally. But I'd had the feeling, even as we bought the house and made plans for a fence and a nursery, that something was slipping out of my fingers and if I didn't grab it back, it would be gone forever. When I had agreed to the idea of a baby, that feeling of loss had passed temporarily and for a while, things between us had been almost like old times.

Almost.

Working with Harvey in the ring had given me a reprieve from my self-blame. Maybe, with Dave, it had been less about a baby and more about me finding my true self.

Either way, I wasn't going to go back to being exactly the way I had been before. For once, that thought didn't terrify me.

"Anyway," the woman said, "we're all glad to see Harvey staying in Dave's family. He's such a part of the dog community." She bent down and patted the dog, who showed about as much response as a fence post. "We love ya, Harv."

With a final sympathetic touch to my shoulder, the woman rose, wished me well, then went off, with Her

Highland Warrior trotting along at her side, clearly not affected by his romance novel nomenclature.

I rose and crossed to the windows, just as the show ended and people streamed out of the hall's doors.

Had Dave been about to give it all up, for me? Or did he have other plans in mind? And when I'd delayed the promise I'd made him, again and again, had that been what drove him back into Susan's arms?

Or was I trying to create shapes out of clouds that were thin and wispy? Trying to frame a picture of a marriage that was still too blurry around the edges to discern any details?

"What do you think, Harvey?" I asked, bending down to the dog. "You have any opinions on what the heck Dave was thinking?"

Poor Harvey's face was as droopy as a limp piece of celery. Maybe he already knew Dave had died. Maybe he'd understood my conversation with the woman.

I unclipped his leash, thinking if I held him, this heavy sadness would lighten. But the second the silver clip slipped out of the circular connection, Harvey bolted, his nails scrabbling against the carpet for purchase, propelling him forward, a tiny furry rocket. He sniffed the air, a canine pinball pinging off the walls, down the hall, back again, searching.

"Harvey!" I cried, taking off after him. The new high heels I'd bought for the show slid against the carpet, catching my step.

The thick crowd of chattering contestants and their pets separated me from the terrier, whose wily body slipped easily under and between the canine and human legs. He was out of sight before I could make my way to the outside perimeter of the people mass. I pushed by a man in a dark suit, still calling Harvey's name, then stopped short.

In the far corner of the room, a door to the outside had been left open. Maybe to release some of the heat in the convention hall. Or maybe left propped open by a security guard sneaking a smoke break. Bright sunshine streamed in across the crimson carpet, blazing a golden path to freedom.

"Harvey!" The word fell on deaf dog ears.

Harvey was gone.

CHAPTER 17

I bent under shrubbery and crawled behind the Dumpsters of the Grand Resort Hotel, ignoring the stench of yesterday's dinner remains, searching for a dog my husband had dumped on me in the afterlife and who had become a weird part of me, of my family. As I did, I could practically hear Patsy Cline singing in my ear, ramping up her chorus.

I was crazy; this whole thing was crazy.

But damn it all, I still loved the man. He'd loved the dog, and other than Susan and Annie, Harvey was the last living tie to Dave. I had no intention of keeping Susan or making a living memorial out of Annie.

But Harvey…

Despite everything, the silly terrier had wormed his way into my heart and suddenly, I wanted him back, wanted to tell him I was proud of him. To thank him for helping me find another side of myself, a side I hadn't even known existed. I wasn't about to run off to Hollywood for a new career, but I was going to live differently when I got home.

And most of all, I wanted to tell Harvey that Dave, if bigamists made it into heaven, was proud, too.

I slithered out from behind a rhododendron, then stopped in the middle of the full, busy parking lot, shaded my eyes and scanned the surrounding area. Congested with shops and hotels, cars and people, it made finding Harvey impossible.

I worried that someone would kidnap him. My heart sank in my chest, tight with panic. Harvey was nowhere to be found.

"Dave," I said to the blue expanse of sky, "why couldn't you have gotten a German shepherd? A malamute? *Anything* bigger than a bread box."

All I got for an answer was a horn beeping at my butt. I wheeled around and faced an elderly woman with a white-knuckled grip on her Mazda's steering wheel, glaring at me and muttering things I was sure I didn't want to hear out of a grandmother's mouth.

I stepped to the side and Grandma zipped by me with a whoosh of smoggy air. I choked and coughed, my eyes watering.

Matt's words came back to me, the story of how Harvey had happened into Dave's life. Had the dog been triggered to run away the first time because his owner had died? Or because his first owner had been the dysfunctional kind who forgot to feed Harvey and saw him more as ornamentation than pet?

Or had Harvey run away that time, and this time, because he'd been paired with a completely inept dog-show stand-in?

I'd been able to run through Harvey's routine, get him to do his tricks, but clearly, I had yet to find a way to connect with him. To make him want to come when I called, not just do it for the Beggin' Strips.

Susan hurried across the parking lot toward me in a little skip step, the kind made possible by three-inch heels. "Did you find him?"

"No. He's so small. He could be anywhere." Guilt washed over me. "What if someone took him?"

"You know Harvey. He's smart. He'd never leave with someone else. Besides, I think he's looking for Dave." Susan drew up beside me, crossing her arms over her ample chest. "What do we do now?"

I wheeled around and faced her. "I don't know, Susan," I said, frustrated more with myself and my inability to find the dog than with her. "I don't know how a dog thinks. I thought I did, but I was wrong." Right then, I was through with being in charge, with trying to reassemble a jigsaw puzzle that got messier by the minute. "You make the plan, Susan. Apparently, you knew my husband better than I did."

I stalked off, anger exploding in my chest like a cheap fireworks display. I blew past Matt, ignoring the question in his eyes, kept walking beyond Vinny, the gathered crowd of speculating attendees, ignoring them all. I headed into the hotel and straight for the bar, the only solution I could think of right now.

"A rum and Coke. Don't bother with the Coke."

The bartender arched a brow but didn't say anything. He did as I asked, pouring some Captain Morgan into a squat tumbler of ice, then floating a twist of lime on the top.

I took a gulp, squinted against the burn of alcohol. I took another drink, squinted a little less. A third, and no squint at all.

I sank onto a stool and sipped at the remaining rum. A sense of peace stole over me, yet, even as it did, I knew it was temporary, brought on by the artificial blanket of alcohol.

That's what I got for leaving my afghan at home.

"There you are." Susan slipped onto the stool beside me and ordered the Coke that was missing from my drink.

I sighed. "Sorry for taking all that out on you. We both lost in this deal."

Susan waved a hand. "Forget it. You're entitled to a little meltdown."

I gave her a weak smile. "A little Dog-Gone-Good frustration."

She smiled back. "Yeah."

"To Dave," I said, raising the glass and clinking it against hers. "And to the mess he left behind."

"Yeah." She knocked back some Coke, slid it over to the bartender and asked him to add some rum. "Seems like a good idea right now."

We drank, neither of us saying anything for a while. "We need to find Harvey," Susan said.

"I agree." A sigh slipped past my lips. "But unless you have dog ESP, I can't even begin to think of where he went."

Susan shrugged. "Why not think like a dog?"

I rolled my eyes. "Now you're starting to sound like my sister."

"I'm serious. If you were Harvey, where would you go?"

"I don't know, Susan," I said, draining the last of the rum from the glass, and signaling to the bartender to get me another. "The pound? A PetSmart store? I have no idea. I've never owned a dog, I'm not a dog, I can't think like one."

"So you're just going to give up?"

I spun on the stool to face her. "Right now, Susan, I am not up to handling this. Why can't *you* crawl around in the shrubbery and find him?"

"Because…I just can't. I'm not like you, Penny." She ran a finger along the rim of her glass, not meeting my eyes. "I can't just go out there and take over."

"Why not? I did it. You think I really wanted to leave my couch and trek halfway down the Eastern seaboard with my dead husband's secret wife and his stage dog? I did it because I knew if I didn't, I'd never know the truth. A truth which, quite frankly, sucks."

"You can handle things like that. I can't."

"But you're sitting right beside me. You went on this trip with me. If I can do this, then so can you," I said, softer now.

"Yeah, but I did it *with you*. Those are the operative words." She took a sip of her drink, toyed with the lime twist. "I'm not the kind of woman who takes the bull by the horns. Heck, I don't even come anywhere near the bull."

"Are you kidding me?" I looked at her, still all neat and pretty in a knee-length black cotton dress, despite the long day. She looked as if she had just stepped off the cover of *Vogue*, not as if she'd been arguing with her husband's primary wife. "You seem so...well adjusted to this whole thing. Here I am, a blubbering mess half the time and you're all sunny-side up."

Susan shrugged and stirred her drink, watching the lime bob among the ice. "It's an act."

"Well then you deserve an Oscar." I took a big sip of my second drink. It went down smooth and easy, too easy.

Susan sipped, silent for a long while. She sighed, then ran her hand across the surface of the bar before she spoke again. "It's all fake."

"What is? The bar? Heck, I'm no carpenter, but even I can tell it's not real wood."

"No, I meant me."

I glanced at her. A beautiful, perfect-featured blonde who could have easily modeled or been Miss USA. The kind of woman other women hated on principle because she'd been gifted with all the things everyone else spent a lifetime Sweatin' to the Oldies to achieve. "Looks pretty real to me."

Susan let out a little laugh, the sound jerking from her with a bitter note. She reached into her purse and pulled out a picture. "That's me, six years ago."

I glanced at the photo, a worn wallet-size picture of a couple. The denim-clad guy was bearded and scruffy, a bandanna wrapped around his temples. Thankfully, he was not my husband.

If Susan hadn't told me she was the woman in the picture, I never would have believed it. Three hundred pounds hung off her frame, made worse by a shapeless denim dress and a pair of Birkenstocks. Glasses hid her blue eyes, and dark brown curly hair obscured most of her face. She wore no makeup and lacked her usual perky smile.

"This is *you?*"

"Yeah." Susan took the photo back and tucked it into her wallet, hiding it behind a Visa. "Before I had my procedure."

"Procedure?"

"Stomach stapling." Susan brightened. "It changed my life."

My own stomach turned over at the thought of someone messing with my internal organs with office supplies. "That's how you lost all the weight?"

"With that, and with a little help from my neighborhood plastic surgeon." She leaned closer and gave her chest a pat. "Like I said, it's all fake."

I couldn't help but look at her perky fauxness. "Did Dave know?"

Susan swallowed and wouldn't meet my eyes. "He paid for it."

"He paid for *plastic surgery*?" The same man who thought we could make our old refrigerator last another year? Who'd told me the only good fences were made out of real wood, not vinyl? Who had insisted we buy organic produce to compensate for his Big Mac addiction?

"He did it for me. So I could feel good about myself," Susan said, now turning an earnest gaze on me. "You don't know what I was like back then. I had all the self-confidence of a flea. I dropped out of high school because of my weight, because of the way kids teased me. I never went to college. I never did anything until I met Dave."

A part of me wondered if my husband had been building the perfect wife, but as I looked into Susan's eyes and thought of the man I knew, I realized he would have done exactly what she'd said. Handed over the cash for whatever would make her happy.

"He encouraged you to do all this?"

"He gave me the belief that I could do it. Dave fell in love with me when I was still heavy. I couldn't believe anyone could love me like that, I mean really love me. Fat or skinny, he didn't care. He saw the real Susan underneath and because of that, it gave me the courage to go for what I'd always wanted. What is it they say on those commercials? To make the outside match my inside. He *did* something for me, Penny. He didn't just write the check." Susan reached over and took my hand. "He was a good man."

I had to look away, to study the dusty velvet image of a bunch of dogs playing poker. I remembered that same picture hanging in our basement when I'd been a kid, dangling from a wire on a nail. My dad and his buddies played poker down there every Friday night because my mother couldn't stand the smell of their smoke, the sound of their laughter. Inevitably, she would claim a headache and head off to bed, leaving my father to both police his daughters and his hand.

Until finally, one day, he'd had enough. My father walked out and never looked back. That night, my mother put the poker dogs picture into the trash, as if she were putting him there, too. She never mentioned the man's name again.

"Did doing all that change you?" I asked, wanting, I guessed, the secret to unlocking the rest of Penny, too.

"It changed how I look. It changed how I acted

when I went out in public. I stopped being a wall-flower. Got my GED, signed up for college. It's just a community college, but it's something. A goal. I'm still going, working on my degree in psychology, but at least I'm moving forward with my life, instead of just watching it from the sidelines."

The words stung, sending a flare of jealousy through me. Why hadn't Dave done that with me?

I raised my glass toward her again. "Then maybe we should toast Dave the saint." The words were bitter, tinged by the alcohol.

"He wasn't a saint, Penny. But I do owe him a lot."

"So go on out there and find his dog," I said, staring into the murky brown rum. I gulped down the last bit, tossed a bill on the bar, then left.

Let Susan pick up the pieces for a while. I was going to find a good blanket and disappear.

CHAPTER 18

I took a cab back to my hotel room, crawled into the uncomfortable, still unmade bed and slept until the rum wore off. When I awoke, it was late afternoon. The sinking sun sliced a sharp edge of orange through the curtains.

Straight into my hungover, regretful face.

Susan hadn't returned to the room. Nor had Harvey found me. Apparently no miracles had occurred in the two hours I'd been asleep.

As tempting as it was to close my eyes again, I swung my feet over the side of the bed, took my second shower of the day and got dressed in jeans and comfortable shoes.

Without the alcohol to numb my feelings, guilt crowded onto my shoulders like a flock of birds straining a telephone line. I'd been mean to Susan, and she'd been nothing but nice to me.

Not to mention, I'd lost the dog. I didn't want to

care about a terrier I hadn't asked for, but damn it all, I did. Somewhere between the Massachusetts state border and the Dog-Gone-Good Show, I'd started seeing him as a part of the Reynolds family.

A part of me. And now he was gone.

Oh hell.

My car, I realized, was back at the conference site. I took another cab back to the Grand Resort Hotel, stopped inside for a huge cup of coffee, then got in the Mercedes. As I put the car in reverse, I leaned over the backseat to watch for pedestrians—

And spied Harvey's little denim personalized backpack. All this time, it had sat there, forgotten and never opened.

I grabbed the strap and hauled it up front with me. The zipper stuck a little, then gave way, spilling an assortment of vinyl toys onto my lap, one fuzzy stuffed bunny that looked well loved by a canine, and finally a silver dog whistle.

Jackpot.

I got out of the car, the stuffed bunny under one arm, the whistle in my other hand. Every few feet, I blew on the silent whistle.

In my haste to find Harvey, I completely forgot

that I was at a dog show. Before I could say toot-toot, I had become the Pied Piper of Dogdom.

From all corners of the conference site, dogs broke away from their masters, dashing to my side, tails wagging. An Airedale brushed up against me, then a Great Dane, crowded in by two collies and a trio of poodles.

I was surrounded by every breed and type of dog— except the one I wanted.

"What the hell are you doing?" an elderly man charged up, clipping a leather leash onto the Airedale. He wagged a finger at the slim silver piece in my hand. "You can't just blow that thing around here. It's dangerous, for God's sake."

"Sorry. I'm looking for my dog."

"You lost *Harvey?*" a woman corralling the poodles said. "How could you?"

"He ran away." Even as I said the words, I realized how it sounded. Like I'd been a bad parent and Harvey had headed for greener pastures.

The gaping mouths and narrowed eyes around me echoed that sentiment. As a dog owner, I was a failure.

Gee, add that to my wife score and I'd won zero and lost two.

Then, I spied a familiar streak of brown and white

slipping under a parked VW Bug. "Harvey!" I broke out of the parking-lot pound and dashed over to the dog, waving the stuffed rabbit, calling his name.

He hesitated for a second, then sprang off his back two paws and galloped toward me. I scooped him up, not realizing until I held his tiny, trembling body against my chest how much I had missed him.

Tears burned behind my eyes. Oh, this silly dog. Who'd have ever thought I'd grow to care about him? Miss him when he left? Stand in a parking lot surrounded by the animal kingdom, blowing on a whistle to find him?

Harvey snuggled against me, working the rabbit out from my grasp. As soon as he had the stuffed toy firmly in his mouth, he sank into my arms, content. I bent down and nuzzled against him.

"You found him."

I turned around at the sound of Matt's voice. "Yeah. I don't think he went that far." I worked the emotion out of my voice.

"He gets a little stressed by the end of one of these things, which is probably why he went looking for Dave. I'm glad you gave him BooBoo."

"BooBoo?"

Matt gestured toward the stuffed pink bunny. "That's his security blanket."

I felt terrible for never opening the bag, never realizing that the dog was more human and had deeper emotional needs than I'd thought. A security blanket, of all things. But with this dog, it made perfect sense.

"I had no idea." I stroked a hand over the dog. The bunny wasn't Dave, but it was all I could give the dog right now. "I understand missing your security blanket. Sorry, Harv."

Matt cocked his head and grinned. "Am I detecting tender feelings for the dog?"

"Maybe." I put my face near the terrier's and received a rough-tongued lick on my cheek. He smelled of shampoo, dog food and in an odd way, Dave, too. "Okay, yeah."

He chuckled. "Harvey does have a tendency to grow on you."

I leaned closer to Matt. "He captured my heart when he shot Cee-Cee."

Matt threw back his head and laughed. "That was good, wasn't it?"

"I think I'm going to incorporate it into his routine." The words promised a future, beyond this show. "I meant, with Vinny."

"Yeah, I get that." He grinned at me. "You were awesome out there, you know. I never knew you had such theatrical ability."

"Thank you," I said, making a half bow. "I'll be here all day, if you want an encore."

"I might just take you up on that," he said. Those words also implied a future. I was glad when he changed the subject and when that intensity left his expression. "Well, now that you've taken the dog world by storm and made Harvey king, once again, of the Dog-Gone-Good Show, what's next on your agenda?"

I drew in a breath, pushing away the triumph of today. I couldn't run from the truth forever. And I knew, deep in my heart, I had to hear it all before I could go back home. No matter how much it hurt or how much worse it could get.

Matt was right. I'd survived a hell of a lot already. A lot more than I would have ever thought I could. Surely, after coaxing a terrier to play a piano and then engaging in a gunfight with a wayward poodle, facing the next obstacle would be a walk through the daisies.

"I'm going to go see Annie," I said, the resolve finally cemented. "But I'm keeping Harvey armed with his little toy pistol. You never know when a dog like Cee-Cee is going to disrupt the whole plan."

CHAPTER 19

We left Pigeon Forge, Harvey in a brand-new crate on my plastic-coated backseat. I'd left the door of the crate open, per Vinny's advice, in case the dog felt like being sociable.

Susan sat beside me, uncharacteristically silent. The green rectangle of a highway sign blaring an upcoming exit for I-81 North loomed over the car, then disappeared.

One way, home. The other way, Annie.

Susan grasped the silver-buckled purse in her lap, her grip as tight as mine had been on the steering wheel a couple days earlier. It seemed like the trip down from Newton was a year ago, not a few days.

"I can't do this, Penny," Susan said. "You have to go it alone."

I eased onto the shoulder, stopped the car and shut it off, then unbuckled and turned in the seat to face her. This didn't sound like the kind of conversation I should have while trying to drive to Cleveland. Behind us, Harvey perched his paws on the front seat, watching the exchange. "What do you mean, go it alone?"

"I mean I'm done. I can't pretend anymore. And I sure as heck can't meet Annie and her little Mother Goose family." She blew steam onto the window, then traced a circle in it, avoiding looking at me and at Harvey.

"I don't want to meet her, either, but I think we have to. We still don't know if Dave married her or—"

"I don't want to know."

The firm finality of Susan's words surprised me. "Why? When we started out you were all gung ho. Even said this was fun."

Ten points for me for not scoffing after I said the word.

"It was. With you. We're kind of the same. But Annie…"

I laughed. "You and I are about as alike as Mutt and Jeff."

Susan let out a chuckle, then sobered and finally turned to face me. "We're both damned good at pretending, aren't we?"

"I'm not pretending anything."

"Uh-huh. And my breasts are real, too."

"Seriously, Susan. I'm not…" My voice trailed off.

I *was* pretending, at least with everyone I met. I'd been acting all along, at the wake, the funeral, on the road trip with Susan, pretending everything was fine, that this would all work out. "Okay, maybe I am," I said finally. "But that doesn't mean that I want to stop this. Or turn around. After everything, I'd rather deal with truth than with what-ifs."

Susan ignored my statement. She unclipped then reclipped the clasp on her purse. "Have you thought about why Dave sought out another woman? Because I sure have. Since I found out about Annie, I've been thinking about it a lot."

"He was a nymphomaniac." Lord knows he hadn't been all that busy in our marital bed in the past two years, but he had surely been busy with Susan. Any man in his right mind would have.

"No, he definitely wasn't that." She laughed. "I know why he wasn't happy with me. I know why I wasn't enough. But still, I never imagined he'd find someone else." Her voice had gotten smaller, each syllable laced with pain.

I sat in the car, silent, listening to the traffic whiz by, sounding like loud zippers being opened again and again.

"It was the baby," Susan said after a long while. "That's what drove him away."

My body froze, veins turning to ice, spine as immovable as Mount Everest. I worked my mouth around the letters, trying three times before I could get the word out. "Baby?"

"I didn't want one. I—" Susan sucked her bottom lip into her mouth and pivoted away from me.

My hand reached out and covered hers. An odd sisterhood, formed by circumstance. No one else in the world understood what each of us felt. Just Susan and me.

And, in the course of this trip, she had become a friend.

"Because of your career?" I asked. "That's why I told him no. I was too busy at work, making my way up the ladder."

"Trust me, my career as a waitress was never anything big. Dave bought me that house and paid for me to go to college. He thought I could be something. Something more." She shook her head. "Anyway, it wasn't because of my job. It was because of this." She swept a hand over her perfect hourglass frame. "I didn't want to undo all that I had worked so hard to create. I was terrified that if I got pregnant, I'd go back to being that other woman, the one society looked at as nothing more than a gigantic, lazy loser."

"I'm sure you wouldn't have—"

"I had an abortion," she said, nearly spitting the words out, as if she were yanking out a splinter. "I chose my body, Penny. I chose these—" she smacked at her chest with her free hand, so hard I expected her to wince "—over my husband. Over the man who had changed my life. Given me a life, really."

"Did Dave find out?"

She nodded, and the pain in her face made me want to take her in my arms, as if I were the mother and she the child, as I had done so many times for Georgia over the years of our childhood. Instead, I went on holding Susan's hand. "I told him, just before he left for that trip to Ohio. We'd fought about it again that day." She paused. "The day he died."

The jigsaw puzzle assembled itself over our heads. Dave, wanting a baby so badly he'd married another woman, only to be rebuffed again. Neither of us spoke for a long time. Harvey put his two front paws on the headrest and nuzzled my cheek. I gave him an absent-minded pat.

"I didn't want a baby, either," I admitted. Susan was the first person I'd ever told the truth to. Always, with Dave, with Georgia, I'd put up the career block, instead of the truth. "It wasn't my job, though that was the excuse I gave Dave, and me. I guess it was easier than saying I was afraid to have a child, because you know Dave, he would have tried to talk me into it." I inhaled, waited as a line of school buses passed us. "I didn't want a dog or a cat or a baby or anything that would upset the perfect order of my life. I worked too hard to escape chaos to want to invite it back into my world again."

"Do you think that's why he kept looking? Because he wanted a child?" Susan's eyes filled with tears. "Is that why he married Annie?"

"I don't know," I said, my voice cracking into the same range as Susan's. "But it sure looks that way."

"I can't go there," Susan repeated, shaking her head now, firming her resolve. "I can't see her, with Dave's baby, knowing I did this. Knowing I wanted my hips and my breasts more than a child. I don't want to know the truth, Penny. I can't handle it."

"Susan—"

"Don't you understand? I am *not* like you. I would never have gone to your house and asked you to come down here, to go meet Matt and Vinny and Annie. I didn't even want Dave's dog. I dumped him on you and ran away. Until you showed up on my porch, I was doing a damned good job of avoiding the whole thing. It's amazing what a lot of time in a mall can do for your psyche."

She let out a little laugh after the words, but the joke rang hollow and empty.

"But, Susan, don't you want to—"

"No, Penny, I don't. At first, this was a big adventure. It seemed like it might be fun. Even…therapeutic. But it hasn't been." She paused. A semi whipped past us so fast it shook the car. Harvey let out a little yip, of either complaint or worry, I wasn't sure. "All I've done in the last few days is think about Dave and about what went wrong in our marriage. And what I did to make it happen."

I sat back against the car door, surprised to hear my own thoughts echoed back. "You never showed it, never said a word."

A wry smile crossed Susan's face. "Like I said, it's all fake."

"Oh, Susan. You're not fake. You're one of the realest people I've ever met."

Her eyes filled with tears and she reached across the front seat, drawing me into a hug. This wasn't like the hugs other women had given me in the funeral home, those reserved sympathy hugs that stayed behind a certain line of decorum. This was a full-out, thank-you-for-being-my-friend embrace. My arms went around her and I clutched her back just as tightly.

What an odd alliance we had formed. Never had I thought when I saw her and her rhinestone-studded shoes at my husband's wake that I would actually grow to like Susan Reynolds. I definitely hadn't thought I'd end up hugging her on the side of a highway in Tennessee.

If I'd been Walt Disney, I couldn't have written a more fantastical ending to this story.

Susan drew back, swiped at her eyes, smearing her perfect makeup. "I'm going home to Rhode Island, Penny, and I'm going to pretend none of this ever happened. It's what I do best."

"That's not healthy, Susan. You have to deal with this eventually." So would I, but I left my own emotional issues out of the conversation. Seemed we had enough angst in the car already.

"No, I don't. Because the only way I know to deal with life and the crap it throws at me is with a box of Krispy Kremes. I won't go back to being that woman. Not even for Dave. Or you."

CHAPTER 20

Georgia kept me company the whole way to Ohio, burning up my cell minutes with a speakerphone conversation that kept me distracted enough that I could forget the purpose of my trip. "Are you sure you don't want me to fly down there and meet you?" my sister said, her voice oddly disjointed from the cell connection. "I could be there in a few hours."

"No, thanks. I need to do this by myself." I was finally back on the road, after dropping Susan at the Knoxville airport and buying her a ticket home. We'd hugged and cried like college roommates, and I'd promised to call her when I got back to Newton.

A part of me was glad Susan was gone. What I'd said to Georgia was true—I *did* need to do this by myself. It was kind of like growing up all over again. I'd started doing that at the Dog-Gone-Good Show, both with Harvey and with Matt.

Now there was a course I could teach: Learning how to be an adult widow in fifteen easy steps.

"You don't have to carry the whole world on your shoulders, Penny," Georgia said, her voice crackling a little as I drove under an overpass.

"I'm not."

"Bullshit. You've been doing it since you were five." On the other end, ice clinked into a glass, followed by the sound of running water. "You became mom and dad and everything in between."

"Dad was gone, Georgia. And Mom…"

"Zoned out."

A moment of silence hummed across the line. "Yeah."

"You know, that might have something to do with all of this. Maybe it's part of why you didn't see what was going on with Dave."

"I didn't see it because he kept it a secret." I refused to become one of those talk-show counseling patients who blamed every adult mistake on my parents being screwed up. I made my own choices, not all of them good, it seemed.

"Nothing's ever a secret, not really. There were signs, Penny. You just chose to ignore them." Georgia's voice was soft with concern, not recrimination. She knew me best, out of everyone in my life, and loved me best, out of everyone in my life.

Nevertheless, it felt odd, after so many years of being the voice of wisdom to Georgia to be hearing the same back from her. Little sisters, it seemed, did indeed grow up. And turn the tables.

"I—" I cut off the denial before it vocalized. I thought back to all the long trips, the weekends when he was suddenly unavailable or he didn't answer his cell phone. Always, Dave had had an excuse. If I'd wanted to, I could have pressed the issue. I just hadn't wanted to, because doing so would have meant inviting Mr. Chaos over for afternoon tea. He was never a very good guest. "I guess I did."

"And don't you think at least part of that is because of what happened when we were kids?"

"Oh come on, Georgia, this isn't an episode of *Oprah*. It's real life. I didn't see what Dave was doing because I wanted my marriage to work."

"And the fact that we were abandoned at three and five by a father who went out for a gallon of milk and never came back had nothing at all to do with that?"

I didn't answer her. Silence filled the space between us.

"All I'm saying is you might want to consider the past as part of your present."

"History repeating itself and all that? Well, my husband did come back. Explain that one."

"He loved you."

I snorted. A Mazda passed me, the driver hitting at least ninety in the fast lane.

"If it wasn't love that kept him coming back, what was it?" Georgia asked.

"It couldn't be love. You don't do this to the people you love."

"Maybe Dave was the kind who loved too much."

I groaned, then moved into the center lane, avoiding a semi rolling up the on-ramp, the driver chatting on his cell, distracted enough that I wasn't going to put the Benz in his path. "Now you're really starting to sound like a self-help book."

Georgia laughed. "That's why they exist. To give me good one-liners. Listen, I could be totally wrong. Just think about it, that's all I'm saying. Give Georgia's words of wisdom a chance."

"I will."

"And when you meet Annie…"

"Yeah?" I prompted when my sister paused.

"Give her the benefit of the doubt. I doubt she's the

evil Witch of the West who absconded with your man. Susan, remember, was just as stunned by this as you were. Apparently cool shoes don't make you smarter."

I chuckled. "She did have some nice shoes. And she wasn't a bad person."

"Oh, damn, Penny. I gotta go. My Reiki appointment is in ten minutes. Now I'll have to rush right over there."

"Isn't the point of Reiki to teach you to be calm?"

"No, the point is for me to visit with the cute instructor and watch his butt whenever he's walking around the room. It's a hell of a vantage point, you know, sitting on the floor on pillows."

I laughed and disconnected the call, then put on my blinker and eased into the lane leading to the next exit, which promised food, gas and a hotel. My stomach rumbled, reminding me that it had been six hours since I'd eaten anything. Not that I expected to find anything remotely healthy at a place labeled Trucker's Oasis, but it was better than passing out at the wheel from starvation.

A red Honda eased in behind me, and followed me all the way off the ramp and into the parking lot of the fast-food restaurant I'd chosen. I swung into a space, then saw the Honda take the space to my right.

Not that unusual for another car to take the space beside me or for two drivers to simultaneously select this restaurant out of the four on the strip, but still…unnerving. I sat in the Benz, clutching my keys, trying to think of what I'd learned in that self-defense class I'd taken with Georgia three years ago. Nothing came to mind. That one, too, had had a cute instructor.

A knock on my window made me jump. I turned, ready to scream for help, when I noticed a familiar face through the window. "Matt?"

Joy fluttered through me, chased by a renewal of the attraction I'd felt for him. They were heady feelings, almost too big to handle.

He grinned and I lowered the window. "I thought you might want some company." His gaze connected with mine, and his green eyes softened, touching a tender vein in me. "You know, to meet Annie."

Not my favorite topic of conversation, not with Matt at least. Every time I was around him, my thoughts scattered down other paths.

"I'm fine on my own. Really." I got out, locked the car, leaving the windows down a bit for Harvey, then turned to go into the fast-food restaurant. "Chicken nuggets."

"What?" Matt said, falling into step beside me, unsolicited. But not turned away, either. To be honest, I was glad for the company.

"I have to get Harvey some chicken nuggets. He really likes them. And then…" I drew in a breath, my attention going to the busy highway, cars whipping by at NASCAR speed.

"You don't really want to meet Annie, do you?" He stepped in front of me to open and then hold the door as I passed through.

"I'm not thinking about what I want." I shivered a bit. Should have worn my jacket, but after all that time in the car, I'd gotten hot and forgotten the spring air was sometimes still nearly winter temperature. "Because I can't have what I want."

Matt took my arm and drew me into an alcove beside a lottery-ticket dispenser. A little hand-lettered and misspelled sign said a ten-thousand-dollar winner had been sold here last week, followed by a full row of exclamation points. "What do you want?"

"My life back. Exactly the way it was." But did I? After the dog show, the sandwiches by the river?

"Living in blissful ignorance?"

"Hey, that's not fair."

"It's true, Penny. Until Dave died, you had no idea what else was going on. Now you know some of it at least." He studied me. "Do you really want to go back to the status quo?'"

"I can't. My husband is dead, remember? Besides, what do you care?" I lashed out, not wanting to have this discussion, not beside a bunch of scratch-off tickets and a Coke display. Not wanting to have it at all, in fact. "If it's Harvey you're worried about, don't worry. He'll keep on being your cash cow."

Matt took a step back, his face paling, looking as if I'd hit him. "I don't care if Harvey ever makes another dime. What I care about is you."

"Me?" I scoffed, but inside parts of me were tingling, both with awareness and a little fear. This was new territory, this interest from a man other than my husband, and I still wasn't sure which way to navigate. "You barely know me."

"I know you deserve more than a life built on lies."

I threw up my hands and walked away from him, pretending to be wildly interested in the potato chip selection. "I don't want to talk about this. I don't want to date anyone or think about another life. All I want right now is to get to Cleveland and get this over with."

Matt shrugged. "Okay."

"Okay what?" I grabbed a bag of Doritos off the shelf, then put them back. I jerked another bag up, my vision too blurred to see the brand. "You're not making the decision for me."

"I meant, okay, I'll go along with whatever you want." He reached out toward my arm, turning me back to face him. Gently, he took the chips out of my hand and replaced them on the wire shelf. "But I don't think this is something you should do alone. You've just lost your husband, found out about an entire secret existence he had, and whether you think so or not, you are still emotionally vulnerable. You need someone in your corner, Penny, before you go to Annie's house."

His words touched that vulnerable spot in me again. I softened, catching his gaze. "And why should that someone be you?"

He reached up, as if he was going to touch my face, then lowered his hand, changing his mind. Disappointment hit me square in the chest. "I care about you and if the circumstances were different, I'd be asking you out on a date, maybe dinner, in a restaurant this time," he said, grinning, "and afterward, to a movie or drinks and dancing in a little bar with pool tables and a live singer who can do a really good Barry White. I'd be doing that, instead of asking if I can tag along while you meet a woman who might be your husband's third wife."

"Asking me to…dinner? Dancing? Drinks?" I stared

at him, so taken aback the words weren't registering. This wasn't just playing around the issue of him being interested, this was out and out flirting.

Matt took a step forward, his eyes locking with mine, leaving no doubt that he meant every word he spoke. "In case you haven't noticed, you are a beautiful, intelligent and spirited woman. Any man in his right mind would want you."

I turned away, staring at the glass-walled rainbow of soda selections, anything but him. Right now, there was enough on my plate without adding in feelings for Matt. But they lodged there, all the same, wanting both to pull him closer and push him away. "Well, the circumstances aren't different. And one man in his right mind *didn't* want me."

"Don't," he said, ignoring a trio of people who headed down the aisle and split like a wave around us. Matt put a finger under my chin and turned my face back toward his. "Don't let what Dave did ruin you. Don't let it keep you from ever caring about another man again. I liked Dave, don't get me wrong, but if he was here right now, I'd slug him for what he's done to you."

My mouth opened. Closed. Opened again, but no sounds came out.

"And if you weren't a grieving widow," Matt went

on, his voice and his gaze intense and true, "I'd kiss you. Because I happen to think you are more than enough woman for one man. Anyone who'd do what Dave did to his marriage, to you, has to be crazy."

"You…you want to kiss me?" I stared at him, dumbfounded. When was the last time a man had wanted to kiss me?

And when was the last time Dave had done more than given me the perfunctory goodbye buss on the cheek? Want curled inside me, taking up residence in a place that had been empty for a long time. Want, not just for a kiss, but for Matt.

"Yeah." The word had a gruff, hungry element and it set my breath on edge.

"Okay," I said, drawing in a little oxygen before moving a half step closer to him, wanting this, wanting him, wanting something for myself for now. "Kiss me."

Matt met my gaze for one long, heated second, then reached up with both his hands, cupping the tender skin along the nape of my neck, drawing my mouth closer to his. He lowered his lips to mine, drifting along them at first, then, when I parted them, he deepened his kiss, playing jazz against a mouth that had, for far too long, been listening to soft rock.

Guilt washed over me, then just as quickly washed

away. Dave was gone, and had been gone, technically, for a really long time. I was under no obligation to remain true to a man who hadn't been true to me.

I wrapped my arms around Matt, the foreign feel of another man's body beneath my palms sending an odd curling sensation through my gut. Muscles rippled beneath my touch, flexing as he moved to take me closer into his embrace. When my pelvis bumped against his, want exploded in my brain as fast and furious as a bomb.

I pulled back, out of his arms, out of the sticky situation I'd just invited into my life, suddenly aware of the dozens of people making their way in and out of the convenience store, walking around and past us as if our public display of affection were merely another offering in the store's vast snack selection.

"I'm not going to say that shouldn't have happened," Matt said, heat burning in his deep green eyes, "because as much as I know I should, I don't feel at all guilty about kissing you."

"Neither do I." The realization flooded me with a new set of emotions, a confusing jumble of guilt that I was still married, or should at least still feel married, and a curious blend of desire.

"You are an incredible woman," Matt said, brushing

a lock of hair off my face and, in that one tender gesture, making me want to cry. "And when you're ready, and if you want, I'd like to pursue this path. See where it goes." He grinned, lightening the mood. "Take you out for some karaoke and see if you can sing like Mariah."

I swallowed. The thought of the future, of anything beyond this day and this minute, still seemed to loom over me, too big a thing to grasp.

"Let's get some chicken nuggets, Matt," I said. "We'll start there."

CHAPTER 21

"Did you warn her that we were coming?" Matt asked a half hour later. We'd eaten our food in the dining area, sitting under a fake ski-lodge roof, the odd decor part of some winter-wonderland theme the restaurant had adopted. We'd chatted about the dog show, the weather, nothing. It was an oddly comforting conversation, a preview of what normal could become. Down the road.

I signaled to take the exit that led to Annie's house. "I wimped out. Left a vague message on her voice mail telling her I was a friend of Dave's and that I had a question about Harvey. I said I hoped she wouldn't mind my stopping by this afternoon."

Matt turned toward me. "What if meeting Annie doesn't fill in the rest of the blanks?"

"It has to." Behind me, Harvey was busy devouring his treat. Chicken crumbs scattered all over the plastic, but I refrained from reaching for the wet wipes.

When Harvey was done, he clambered over the seat and plopped his butt between us. He looked from one to the other, tail wagging, clearly overjoyed at the additional traveling companion.

"What if it doesn't?" Matt asked again.

"Then I—" Do what? There was no Plan B. I couldn't go back to the status quo, because that didn't exist, and besides, I'd kind of dramatically changed the status quo back there among the Ruffles.

I also couldn't go back to pretending none of this had happened, because it had. I couldn't go back to having that naive belief in my marriage, because all that had been shattered the minute Susan showed up at the wake.

I looked down at Harvey, now sitting on my lap as I drove, watching the world go by with an excited, panting fascination. And most of all, I couldn't give Harvey away to some stranger, because the silly dog had grown on me.

I drew in a breath, held it tight in my chest, listening to the thud of my heart. "I don't know where to go from here. And that scares me. I've never been the kind of person who was good with spontaneity. I like to know the ending before I start at the beginning, if that makes sense. I like to have all the variables laid out, so I can plan ways to avoid them."

"Well, that idea was shot to hell this week," Matt said. "Nothing like a dog show and a crazy poodle to upset an apple cart."

I laughed a little, then went on, sobering to the reality facing me with each passing mile. "I know I have to go back and find the will, which I bet he kept at his office, because my sister couldn't find it in the house. But I'm not ready to do any of that yet. There's undoubtedly going to be consequences from the estate, and I'll need to deal with those. But before I can get to those, I need to meet Annie, to rule out that last variable. Then, I think I can finally make a plan." Just the thought of the word gave me comfort and undid a tiny bit of the tension in my stomach.

Matt chuckled. "I don't know about all that planning and variables thing. If you ask me, you aren't the same Penny I met three days ago. I don't think you're going to be able to go back home and lay out this little map for the future. I mean, you had a gunfight with a terrier and a psycho poodle in front of several hundred people. Does that sound like a woman who runs her days by a checklist?"

We approached the next turn on the laid-out route from MapQuest. "Annie's house isn't much farther," I said, ignoring his comment for now.

As much as I'd been excited by the turn of events at the dog show, and the way it brought out a spontaneity gene I hadn't even known I had, I was also scared by it. If I wasn't the Penny I used to be, then who was I? And how on earth would I find my way back to normal if I changed too much?

The rest of the turns came quickly one upon the other, shifting the conversation into direction giving, with Matt reading the MapQuest route and me following it. We passed down neat, well-tended streets in a middle-class neighborhood of Cleveland. Middle America, clear in its perfect lawns and bikes haphazardly left in smooth, grass-edged driveways. Two more rights, and then we left the manicured lawns and headed into a part of town that was more run-down, less middle-class perfection. I could practically see the income levels dropping as each block passed.

"Take a right here," Matt said.

"Into the trailer park?" I asked. "I thought Annie had five kids. How can she fit them all into one of these things?" I gestured toward a single trailer at the head of the park. The mobile homes were jammed in together like piano keys.

As I drove and took in one run-down aluminum, portable home after another, I refused to feel sympathy for another of Dave's wives. Heck, I'd already made one a friend. I didn't need another. Next thing I'd know, this whole fiasco would be a Goldie Hawn movie with her and her extra wife buddies singing show tunes as they walked off into the sunset.

The trailer at 2121 Winterberry Lane was a double-wide fronted by a bed of purple crocuses surrounding a small white wrought-iron bench. It had a fresh coat of paint or siding or whatever they did to spruce up the outside of one of these. A new wooden porch led us up to the front door, the wood still holding that fresh-cut smell. Dave had to have paid someone to do this, because he had all the woodworking skills of a monkey.

I held Harvey tight to my chest, my free hand raised to knock. Matt stood beside me, a six-foot dose of moral support.

Inside I could hear the sound of children, their happy voices ringing with laughter, echoed by the barking of a dog. Harvey perked up in my arms, yipping, as if he, too, were joining in.

Traitor.

Susan's words came back to me. What if Dave's baby was in Annie's arms, right on the other side of the flimsy door? What would I do? Say?

Before I could change my mind, I knocked. It was

a good two minutes and a second knock before anyone came to the door.

"Hi, Harvey!" A three-year-old girl stood at the door, her curly brown hair a jumbled riot framing her face and curious brown eyes staring out of a jelly-smeared face. It took her a second to register that there were people holding the dog. "Hi. I'm Holly."

"Hi, Holly," I said, offering up what I hoped looked like a nonthreatening smile as she reached forward and petted Harvey, clearly familiar with him, and he with her. He turned his head and licked her palm, eliciting a giggle. "Is your mother home?"

"Oh, jeez, Holly, how many times do I have to tell you not to open the door to—" A petite dark-haired woman stepped in front of the little girl. Her mouth stopped midsentence and dropped open. "It's you."

The last thing I had expected was for Annie to recognize me. "You know who I am?"

She nodded slowly. "Uh, Holly, why don't you and your sister go make a card for Grandma?"

"I wanna see Harvey. And we made Gramma a card yesterday." The word came out more like *yed-er-day*.

"Well, she'd love another. You know how bored she gets in the hospital. You can see Harvey later." Annie shooed the little girl away, then grabbed a coat that must have been hanging by the door and slipped outside, leaving her front door ajar. "Let's sit at the picnic table and talk. Away from the zoo."

"Your kids will be okay?"

"Trust me. They'll find me if someone gets hurt or takes a toy from someone else. Kids are better than bloodhounds at tracking down a mother." As she walked down her stairs and a few feet across the yard, she gave Harvey a greeting pat.

We slipped onto opposite sides of the picnic table. I studied Annie for a second. She was short, maybe only five foot two, and had spiky dark-brown hair. She wore no makeup, a well-worn button-down denim shirt and black leggings. She looked about as much Dave's type as Susan had.

I introduced Matt, then handed him Harvey's leash. "Do you mind?"

"Not at all," he finished, leaving me with a smile before taking the dog on a walk.

"I'm Penny," I said. "But I guess you already know that?"

Annie nodded. "I wondered when you'd find out about me."

"I didn't. It was…sprung on me. After Dave died."

Annie gasped. "He died?"

"A week ago on Thursday." It was now Saturday afternoon. I'd been a widow for nine days. It felt like nine years.

"Was it his heart? I was always telling him he needed to watch that."

I bit back a renewed sense of jealousy and swallowed one more bit of evidence that I had been completely oblivious to what had been happening with my husband. I'd never worried one bit about his heart. He worked in insurance, for Pete's sake. Probably one of the least stressful jobs on the planet.

Only, it appeared, if you actually *worked* in insurance instead of working with a performing dog and a trio of wives. "Yeah, it was a heart attack."

Tears filled her eyes. She bit her lip and looked away, her knuckles whitening with her tightened grip on the wooden table. I felt like hell. Why was I the one to deliver this news? Why couldn't that friend from the dog show have called her? Or someone else in this supposedly tight-knit community of canine fans have done it?

"I guess that's why Betty called me twice," Annie said with a sigh. She shook herself, as if pushing the emotions to the side, to deal with after the kids went to bed. "I've been busy with the kids. One of them had strep and then the dog ate a wheel off a Tonka truck, so I've been cleaning up puke all week instead of answering the phone."

"Oh." I wasn't sure what she wanted me to say to that.

She laced her hands together, then laid them flat on the table, studying her short, cropped, plain nails for a second. The triplet to my ring glistened in the sun, but on Annie's right hand instead of her left. I didn't bother asking her what jokes Dave had told during the wedding or whether there was a black Benz parked in her carport.

Those were answers I already had.

"I suppose you're wondering how I knew about you," she said. "And why we were involved."

"It has crossed my mind."

"My mother is sick. Has been for a long time. She's got heart disease, which is why I rode Dave about all those damned burgers."

I swallowed hard. I'd never said a word about his fondness for fast food. Chalk one more up for the worst-wife award. "I don't understand what that has to do with Dave and me and—" I spit the word out "—you."

"And Susan," she added.

"You knew about Susan?"

Annie nodded. "I knew it all. I'm smarter than the trailer makes me look."

"I never thought—"

"You don't have to. Anyone who sees me, a single mom with five kids, living in a trailer park, thinks one of two things—white trash or welfare tramp. Heck, I'm a walking government statistic." Annie shook her head. "I'm not here to burden you with my story. Let's just say I made a few bad choices in men and they always left me to pick up the tab."

Annie was a gruffer woman than either Susan or I. Dave couldn't have picked three more different women if he drew our names out of a bride lottery.

"I had a feeling from the beginning with Dave, that he had a wife. But I ignored it." Annie flicked a piece of wood off the picnic table and onto the ground. "Because I was being selfish and I needed him."

Those words sat hard in my stomach, adding to the enormous pile of digested words and secrets already there. Any more of this and I was going to need liposuction. "Because he took care of you?"

Annie let out a little laugh. "Dave? No. He wasn't here long enough to do anything worthwhile. I think he changed a lightbulb once. He played with the kids. Oh, boy, did he love those kids, but he didn't help me."

"Then what did you need him for?" I didn't add any polite apology about butting into her personal life. I figured with Annie, that kind of social dance wasn't necessary. Besides, Dave was my husband and I had a right to know.

Annie drew in a breath, then met my gaze head-on. "Money."

"You didn't marry him for love?"

She scoffed. "No. And he knew I wasn't involved with him for love. I mean, I liked him, but I wasn't *in love* with him. Besides, Dave wasn't looking for love, either. He told me he already had that."

I didn't ask her to fill in the blank of the sentence with a name. Some things, I didn't want to know. Matt had called it blissful ignorance, but when it came to whether my husband had loved me, I preferred to keep on thinking that he had.

"My mother is sick, like I said," Annie went on. "She owns this dress shop, which is where I work. Third generation, a pretty good operation and the pride and joy of my mother's life. But between helping her in the hospital and running the shop, things started getting a little hairy. Business was down, and I'm not exactly management material, as you can tell by the wild animals back in the house." She laughed a little and gestured toward the continued sound of play coming from the trailer. A little boy peeked his face out from behind a curtain, then disappeared for a second before doing it again. "I wasn't making enough money to hire someone in, and I was losing the business. If I'd done that, it would have killed my mother. She started there when she was a little girl, working with my grandmother.

"Anyway," Annie went on, "it was all kinda crashing down on me at once. The mortgage payments for that palace—" again she gestured toward the trailer, where the little boy was still playing peekaboo "—the lease for the shop, the stress of trying to come up with something to make it all work, and then covering the part of my mother's bills that insurance didn't pay."

I put all this together in the mental file I'd been keeping, adding it to what I already knew. "Then why did you do the UKC dog show?"

Annie chuckled. "I'm one of those people who gets a hair up her butt about something and then takes off on a tangent. Last year, it was making a star out of Max. Lord knows the damned dog costs enough, between the dog food and the vet. He might as well earn his keep."

"Did the kids go with you?" I had yet to ask whether one of the five was Dave's. I was working my way up to that question.

"Are you kidding me? Bring them with me? Try taking 'em to a Kroger and see how much fun they have with the canned goods." She laughed, the kind of laughter of someone who knew a world no one else in the room did. "No, I left them home. My best friend Carol offered to take the kids, to give me a weekend away. She's got four of her own, so she's already a little insane. I wasn't going to miss an opportunity for some time alone. It's been a hell of a year." Annie ran a hand through her hair and as she pushed back the brown locks, I could see the tension around her eyes, etched into the dark circles. The sympathy I'd refused to feel bobbed to the surface of my heart all the same. "The kids had taught Max some tricks. They got their hands on some book one time and had him doing all kinds of things. I thought maybe he was good enough to earn some prize money." She shrugged. "It seemed a safer bet than Vegas."

"But Max wasn't all that cooperative and Dave stepped in to help you," I said, filling in with what Vinny had told me.

She nodded. "I should have sent my oldest. She can get that dog to stand on his head, for God's sake. The dog wouldn't obey me at all at the show." She rolled her eyes and glanced again at the trailer, where for now, all had become quiet. I heard the strains of a children's television show. "I don't know why I thought the dog would listen to me. Hell, the kids don't."

Once again, I was struck by how different Annie was from what I'd expected. Coarse around the edges, frank and direct, she wouldn't have been in the top one hundred of women I would have pictured Dave going for.

"Anyway, Dave saw me struggling with that moose and he helped me, even offered a few private lessons. Not because he wanted me," Annie hastened to add, "but because he liked Max. I guess he saw him as a challenge or something. And Harvey and Max got along really well, too."

Somehow, that was easier to take than Dave falling madly in love and using the dog as a ploy to get closer to Annie. It fit the husband I had known, a man who was always off helping people, even when that help-fulness gene cut into our vacations or made him late for work or a dinner party we were supposed to attend. For once, some of the pieces were aligning with what I had believed to be true. "When did you marry Dave?"

Annie drew in a breath, then reached into the pocket of her sweatshirt and pulled out a package of light cigarettes. "Do you mind if I smoke?"

I shook my head.

"I know," she said, as she lit the cigarette, then took a drag. "I have no business lecturing anyone about heart disease when I've got one of these in my mouth. To tell you the truth, they're my excuse for a few minutes of peace. I can go outside on the porch, have one of these and then feel ready to face two more hours in there."

I glanced again at the trailer, which had started up again, the pacifying effects of the TV done with the show. An older boy, maybe about eleven, popped his head out the door. "Mom, will you please tell Carly to get out of my room?"

"Carly, get out of his room," Annie shouted back at the trailer. "Did it work?"

"No. She's still in there. She's trying on my shirts, Mom. She's calling my clothes her costume gallery or something dumb like that. Can we just put her up for adoption?"

Annie heaved a sigh, then rose. "Can you wait a sec? I have to go do some crowd control."

I nodded, then waited as she ground out the cigarette, went inside, apparently resolved the situation, then came back out.

"I have a mutiny on my hands here," Annie said. "Do you want to come in for some coffee? My yard time's over."

We headed into the trailer, Annie ushering me into a seat in the small kitchen at the front. The messy, congested trailer was a mirror of the pandemonium I'd seen at the Dog-Gone-Good Show, only taken up a notch and involving small children. Max the dog was running between the kids as they alternately wrestled, leaped off the sofa and had a play knife fight with weapons made of cardboard.

None of them looked like my husband. None of them looked young enough to be his, given the timeline with Annie. Relief edged around my senses.

Annie disappeared down a hall and must have dispensed some justice, because a preteen girl in too-tight jeans came stomping into the living room. "Why do mothers exist?" she asked of no one in particular, throwing up her hands and letting out a huff.

Annie came out behind her. "To drive their kids crazy." She laughed, then placed a kiss on the girl's head, a kiss that was brushed off, but not before I saw a quick smile take over Annie's daughter's face.

"Okay," Annie said on an exhausted breath as she entered the kitchen. "Coffee. And lots of it." She headed over to the counter and began filling a coffeepot with ground beans.

"Who are you?" The little girl who'd answered the

door stood in front of me, her hands clasped over her belly, which jutted out beneath a striped shirt that she'd probably outgrown a year ago.

"I'm…" I paused. This was a little more complex than I wanted to get into with a kid who still watched Mr. Rogers. "I'm, ah…"

"She's a friend of Dave's," Annie intercepted. "Remember? The nice man who got Max to sit?"

"Oh. Okay. I'm Holly," she told me a second time, then darted off to play with some dolls that were piled up at the end of the sofa.

Dave was known as the nice man who'd trained Max? Not Annie's husband?

"She's the informant. The other kids always send her in because she's the cutest and the youngest." Annie grinned, then sat in the opposite chair while the coffeepot perked behind her. "Now, what else do you want to know?"

Holly was the youngest. She couldn't be Dave's, which meant he and Annie had never had a child together. Two emotions hit me at once—relief and regret. Relief that Annie hadn't been the one to supply what Susan and I had not, and regret that the Dave Reynolds line had ended with him lying naked in a hotel room.

I lowered my voice, particularly with Holly only a few feet away. "Why did you marry him?"

Or rather, why had he married her? But that question tread a little too close on the side of rudeness, so I kept it to myself.

Annie chuckled. "Right to the point, huh? Well, I was in a mess and Dave offered a way out."

"A way out?"

"Business in trouble, five mouths to feed— though the way my kids eat, there are days it seems like ten—and then my mother, needing a place to go once her surgery was done. Rehab is not cheap and those insurance wackos hate to pay for it. As if rehab doesn't help prevent costs down the road." Annie waved a hand. "Don't get me started on the faults of the insurance industry. Honestly, there were days when Dave and I could have one hell of a rousing argument about the deficiencies of the health-care industry."

I waited, not saying anything, still not seeing how any of this added up to her wearing that ring on her finger.

"So anyway, Dave said if we got married, it might make things easier on me. Besides the money, he said it would give the kids a name, get the child-welfare people off my back to produce the various sperm donor's vital stats." Annie leaned forward, lowering her voice. "And that's what most of those jerks were, you know. Sperm donors and nothing else. Because that was the only useful damned thing any of them left me."

"He married you to give the kids a name?" For a second, I thought it was such an odd reason, but then realized Dave—the man who had given our neighbor Tim the lawn mower because Tim's broke the day he lost his job, the man who had sponsored some kid in Ethiopia even as I warned him it was probably a scam—would have done exactly that.

"My kids, I'd do anything for them," Annie said, a softness coming into her eyes. "I know I seem like the worst mom in the world, but try living with these five and see how chipper you are. Still, they're mine and I love them. A couple of 'em have one last name, the others all have mine. I did have one ex-husband," Annie said, the word clearly sour on her tongue. She shook her head, then went on, clearly just as much of a talker as Susan. "Anyway, once we got to talking and Dave heard the whole story of my crappy life, he offered to help me get the business back on track. Pump in some money, help cover the costs for my mother. But most of all, he was there when I went in to deal with those insurance jerks because they were really fighting that rehab thing. He went to bat for me and my mother, really did. Got coverage for twice as many months as I was asking for. And he pumped in enough money to save the family business. Real Disney ending on that one. Things are booming at the shop and my mom should be back to work this summer."

"And not to mention, Dave trained Max for you."

"Yeah, he did. That dog is a regular performer now. A couple times a year, I bring him to those shows and he does good. Not nearly as well as Harvey, but he's got some talent chops on him."

I considered this new information. It all made sense now. The check, the way everyone who knew about Annie seemed to be protective of her. She had been a woman in dire straits and my husband, whom I could either love or damn and right now I was doing both, had stepped in to play the white knight. "Wait. Why doesn't Holly know who Dave is?"

"Because I'm not the heartless witch I look like." Annie patted at her pocket for her cigarettes, then changed her mind. She rose, poured us each a cup of coffee and returned to the table. "I never married him."

My mug was halfway to my mouth but I never took the sip. "You…you never married him?"

"No. I mean, we were going to. Had a date and a

witness and the paperwork all done for the court-house, but at the last minute, I backed out."

"Because you found out about me?"

"No. I didn't know about you and Susan when Dave proposed." Annie reached across for my hand and met my eyes. "That's the God's honest truth, Penny."

I believed her. If there was one thing Annie was, it was honest. There was no pretension, no fancy shoes and boob jobs hiding her true self from the world. She was the kind of woman who thrust it all out there and basically told you to take it or leave it. "What made you back out?"

She sighed. "Dave would have made it all easy. One *I do* and all my problems would be solved. He is…" She paused, then corrected herself. "He *was* the kind of guy a lot of women would sacrifice their right arm to meet. Compassionate, funny, giving. Would bend over backward to make sure you were happy. But… that was the whole problem." Annie's attention went to the window. "He wasn't enough of a jerk."

"You couldn't take advantage of him." My esteem for Annie went up a few notches. Damn it, now I was beginning to like her, too. My husband, I supposed, had had good taste in people.

Annie swallowed and her eyes misted. "No, I

couldn't. The Catholic guilt would have killed me. But I kept the ring—" at that, she twirled the diamond on her right hand around "—because I kept hoping. You know, that some fairy tale would happen and we'd both fall madly in love. Then we could run off into the sunset while I left the kids with a sitter."

"How did you find out he was already married?"

"I put the pieces together. He didn't live here, didn't have a home anywhere nearby. Vinny called once and mentioned something about Dave just getting back from Rhode Island when he'd told me he was going to Colorado. I told you, I've been with a lot of liars." Annie shrugged. "I just knew. So I confronted him and he told me, even showed me a picture of you. I think he needed to tell someone. He'd been keeping it from everybody. You, Susan, Matt, Vinny. I'm not even sure Harvey knew."

"I had no idea," I said softly, embarrassed to admit it but somehow needing to tell her. "I never put any pieces together."

"Honey, you were the one Prince Charming married first. You think Snow White ever wondered if there was something going on outside the castle, after all that man did to be with her?"

I laughed a little. "No, probably not."

"Besides, you don't look the type to date losers from hell. You have to have personal experience with those kind of guys to develop the nose." She spread her hands, indicating herself. "Dave wasn't a loser, I don't mean that. But he was a guy who was…confused. The thing he liked most about me, he said, was my family. Loved the kids. Maybe he was looking for that, I don't know. We never got that far."

I nodded, thanked her for the coffee, then rose. "Thank you, Annie."

She reached for my hand and gave it a squeeze. "One day, I asked him who it was he loved and he said it was you. I don't know what drove him to complicate things like this."

I knew that answer. I swallowed, then met her gaze. "I wasn't that good of a wife. I wouldn't have children, I wouldn't let him bring home a dog."

"Don't keep blaming yourself. If Dave really wanted all those things, he would have worked on it with the woman he already had." She paused, her focus going to some far-off place. Tears shone in her eyes, grief bubbling up to the surface. An instant later, Annie had swiped it away. "Some men, they keep grabbing for the new toy because it's easier than trying to fix the one they already have."

CHAPTER 22

My goodbye with Annie was far less emotional than it had been with Susan. She was holding one kid on a hip, while yelling at another who had started coloring on Max's head with a Sharpie marker.

Annie had been right—June Cleaver she was not.

"You take care," Annie said, embracing me with one arm. "Carly, quit that! Oh, wait, Penny. I have something for you." She ducked back into the trailer and returned a moment later with a box. "Carly, you draw glasses on that dog and you'll never watch TV again!" She leaned forward and handed the box to me. "Dave left this behind, last time he was here. He always had it with him when he traveled. I never looked inside it, though. Figured if he wanted me to know, he'd tell me." A bittersweet smile crossed her face. "Guess it's true that all the good ones are gone, huh?" She sighed and studied me for a long second while the kid on her hip tugged at her hair. "Anyway, you have a safe trip. It's time for the warden to go back to work."

I met Matt outside, where he'd been waiting at the picnic table, having left Annie and I alone to talk the whole time. Harvey was at his feet, tired but playing a little with Holly, who had climbed into the dirt under the table to play with the dog. Annie called for Holly from inside the trailer, her voice reaching decibels I hadn't thought possible for humans.

As Holly went back inside, with one last sad look at Harvey, I sat down beside Matt, suddenly just as tired as the terrier.

"How'd it go?" he asked.

"Not so bad. I think I'm at the end of Dave's wives. Or, I hope I am." I ran a hand over the box, wondering what it held. More answers?

Or more questions?

I already had enough of those to host a Dave version of *Jeopardy!*

"You ready to go?"

I nodded. "It's time to go home. Try to put my life back together. Figure out the assets, the division of the estate." I inhaled, then let it go. "In other words, move forward."

"You've done a lot of that already."

I glanced over at him and thought of the kiss back

in the convenience store. "Yeah, I have." I grinned. "And I have the dog trophy to prove it."

He laughed, then loaded us all into the car, taking the wheel and giving me some time to nap. The miles between Annie's and where we'd left Matt's car passed quickly, almost too quickly. I had started to like Matt, to like him in a way I hadn't liked anyone in a long time. That both scared and excited me.

I figured it was one of the things I could put on a shelf and deal with later. After I'd had some time alone to think, to discover who Penny Reynolds was—

Without Dave, but now with a dancing, singing Jack Russell terrier.

We reached his rental car and parked a couple of spaces away. Both of us got out of the Benz and stood beside the red Honda in the awkward silence that came at the end of a date. Only this wasn't a date and I wasn't expecting a good-night kiss.

Was I?

Right now, after the week and a half I'd had, I had no idea what I wanted. I don't think I was even capable of ordering an ice cream at Dairy Queen.

"You going to be okay?" he asked me. "It's a long drive back to Massachusetts. If you want, I can drive your car and you can take my plane ticket, change the New York to Boston."

I thought of the Penny I had been before this journey. I'd avoided conferences because they upset my schedule. I'd planned every trip I ever took, even if it was just to the grocery store, to make the best use of my time and to take the least stressful route. Everything in my life had been scheduled and regimented because if I kept it all on a tight leash, I felt I could fend off some unpredictable disaster.

It turned out, of course, that I hadn't been controlling a damned thing.

Now, I was living more or less by the seat of my pants. I glanced over at my car, where two maps I'd printed the day before sat on the dash. Each from Internet sites that provided turn-by-turn guidance and exact distances and times for my journey back up to the East Coast, the main one and the backup, should something happen to the first copy. I might be loosening up, but I had no intentions of getting lost.

"I'll be fine," I told Matt, and as I said the words, I finally felt as if they might be true. I no longer had the urge to curl up under the afghan and shut out the world for a month, a year. "I'll get a motel or something along the way, rather than try to drive it straight through."

"Good." Matt stood there, his keys in his hand, looking as if he wanted to say something more. His gaze connected with mine and a surge of attraction rose inside me. "Are you sure you're going to be okay, Penny? I mean, emotionally."

I scanned the traffic rushing by us, the deep green of new spring grass along the side of the road, the bright blue April sky punctuated by a burst of orange sun. The world had gone on despite my husband dying and the surprise of his near-triple bigamy. And so, too, would I. "Yeah, I'll be okay."

He gave me one quick kiss, a noncommittal, non-rushing-things kiss. I appreciated that from him, as well as the way he cupped my cheek at the end, studied my eyes, and gave me the grin that had become as familiar as Harvey.

It took me a day and a half to get back home. As promised, I spent the night in a Motel 6 along the way, falling into a deep, dreamless sleep that felt more re-storative than a bottle of One A Day.

I spent the drive back with Harvey nearly glued to my side, his little BooBoo the only thing that sepa-rated us. I knew why—he was missing Dave and clinging to me helped fill that void.

And keeping my hand on his little head as I drove

through miles and miles of unfamiliar land did the same for me.

All those hours alone in the car allowed me to do the one thing I had yet to do—grieve. Memories of Dave flooded my mind, tumbling one on top of the other, like a bunch of children all seeking to be the favorite.

All the bad ones came first, released by the remains of the betrayal still simmering inside me, but then as I drove, a calmness descended onto my shoulders. The bad memories yielded to the good ones:

The day he surprised me with the Benz, wrapping the entire car in a festive balloon-decorated paper. The first Christmas we celebrated, when Dave had brought home a tree so big we had to move the sofa out of our tiny apartment living room to make room for its massive green circumference. The day we bought the house, when he insisted on carrying me across the threshold, then nearly dropped me when he tripped.

There were dozens of memories, small, big, all of them part of the fabric of our marriage. I played them back on my mental movie screen, searching for where the threads had unraveled.

But I was tired, emotionally, physically, in every way, and connecting the dots seemed too big a job right now. Tomorrow would be time enough to find those loose ends and hopefully tie them back together.

Georgia was waiting when I got home, sitting on my porch in the dark, wrapped in an old tattered quilt I kept in the wooden chest beside the swing.

"Georgia!" I said, getting out of the car, Harvey and his little bunny in one arm, my overnight bag dangling from the opposite hand. "You didn't have to wait for me to get home. It's so late."

She hurried down the driveway, wrapping me and Harvey in a hug. "Of course I did. I'm your sister."

I hugged her tight, tighter than I ever had before, drawing comfort, a sense of home, of place, from the sister who had oftentimes been more like a daughter than a sibling. The scent of berries and clean cotton rose off her skin, sweet and soft. "It's good to see you."

She pulled back and studied me. "You've changed."

I smiled. "For the better, I hope."

Georgia nodded. "Much better. You seem stronger, more independent." She grinned. "More spontaneous."

Weariness descended over me. "I'm not feeling very spontaneous right now, not after all that time on the road."

Georgia took my overnight bag out of my hands, then waved me toward the walk. "Then let's hurry and get you inside. You'll feel much better with a glass of wine in your hands."

A few minutes later, the two of us were sitting on the sofa, my shoes kicked off and forgotten by the front door, a mess I would have never let stood before. In light of the past few days and all the changes I'd been through, though, making sure my shoes were neatly lined up in the hall closet didn't seem quite so important.

"So, what was Annie like?" Georgia asked.

"Nice, but a little rough around the edges. I liked her. Very much." I took a sip of the white wine Georgia had brought over, a blend that wasn't too sweet or too dry. For a second I could believe Georgia was compromising her tastes with mine. Then I caught a glimpse of the cartoony apples dancing around the label. It seemed Georgia's method of picking libations wasn't so bad after all. "I liked Susan, too. Both of them were women I wouldn't mind having as neighbors. Even friends."

Georgia shook her head. "Who would have thought that when this whole thing began?"

"Not me. *Definitely* not me." I absentmindedly patted Harvey, who had curled up beside me on the cushion, his little body directed toward the crackling fire I had lit a few moments before. "It's like... Oh, this is going to sound silly."

"*You* sound silly?" Georgia said, sitting back with a bemused expression on her face. "Please indulge me, big sister."

"It's like Dave was Goldilocks and we—me, Susan and Annie—were the three bears. One was too pretty, one too tough and one was—" I cut off the words. I hadn't been just right. If I had been, he wouldn't have looked at the other bears.

There went my fairy-tale theory. Good thing I wasn't writing for the Brothers Grimm.

"One *was* just right, but Dave was too busy looking for more that he couldn't see how perfect you were." Georgia took a sip, then placed the goblet on the end table. "After meeting them, why do you think he wanted to marry Susan and Annie?"

"I think..." I dug for the truth that had occurred to me on the long, solitary, memory-filled drive home. "I think Dave needed to be needed. If there was one thing Susan and Annie gave him, it was that."

"And you, superwoman of the year, did not?"

"No. I was all self-reliant and smart. Or so I thought. Looking back, I see that I wasn't nearly as strong as I'd imagined. This whole trip terrified me."

"Yeah, but you made it. That's strength."

I sipped at my wine, waiting for the smooth drink to make its journey down my throat. "I hid all my worries from Dave because I thought he needed me to be strong."

"The perfect wife, huh?"

"Something like that." A burst of laughter escaped me. "How far from the truth was that? Here I thought I had it all in the palm of my hand, and really, I was just being blind."

"What else happened?" Georgia rose to get another glass of wine, then returned to the sofa. "Because I get the sneaking suspicion you did more than meet the other women and take Harvey through his routine."

"Oh, yeah." I toyed with my wineglass, running a finger along the rim. "I kissed Matt, for one."

"The dog's agent?" Georgia slapped my knee. "You kissed *him?*"

"Actually," I admitted, heat filling my cheeks at the memory, "I asked him to kiss me. In a convenience store, next to the snack foods."

Georgia placed the back of her palm on my forehead. "No fever. Okay, what have you done with my sister?"

"I took your advice, that's all, and I let go of the pier for a little while."

"Good for you!" Georgia squealed. "So tell me, is something going to happen with him?"

"Maybe." It was too hard a question to answer right now. "If it does, it'll be down the road. I need time to be just Penny. To see where and who I am. And how I'm going to live this new life." I drew in a breath, let it out. On the mantel, Dave's picture looked back at me, the right-hand twin to mine. Three years ago, we'd had them done, as Christmas presents to each other. I'd stood behind the photographer as she snapped Dave's, which had made him look at me instead of the lens. In that portrait, I saw love in his eyes. "Plus, Dave wasn't the villain here. It takes two to ruin a marriage."

Georgia's brows knit together in confusion. Leave it to my sister to see me as the hero. "You? What do you think you did?"

I laughed. "Gee, take a look around the house and I think it's pretty clear. I was too rigid, too set in my ways and too resistant to anything that came close to looking like change."

"Like the idea of having a baby with Dave." Georgia's voice was soft with understanding.

I nodded, willing away the tears that sprang to my eyes. "Yeah, like that."

A long silence passed and my sister, the only one

who knew the whole story of the Penny who lurked behind the lists and organized shelves, studied my face, reading my thoughts as easily as a novel. "You didn't want to be a mother ever again, did you?"

"I couldn't make that mistake a second time." The words lodged thick in my throat.

"Aw, Pen, it wasn't a mistake. It was an accident. And you did nothing wrong." Georgia looked at me and took one of my hands in both of hers. "You were so good with me, all those years, I can't imagine that if you were given a second chance, you wouldn't have been, or even still be, a great mother to your own kids."

"Georgia, I can barely take care of this dog!" Harvey started at the sharp notes in my voice and I ran a hand down his back to soothe him. "Besides, I was never mother material. Look what happened with—" I couldn't finish that sentence. Heck, I'd left it unfinished for nearly twenty years.

Georgia grabbed both of my arms and forced me to look at her, seeming stronger than my little sister had ever been. "It was not your fault, Penny. Things happen. Things go wrong every day."

I broke away from her and stood, facing the fire, pretending I needed to warm my hands. "I don't want to talk about this."

"When are you going to?" Georgia said, rising to stand beside me. "You have to someday."

"Do you want to know why my baby died?" I said, wheeling on her, unable to hold back the emotions that had waited in some secret corner of my mind for two decades. Undealt with, untalked about, because I had stuffed them away as quickly as they had popped up. "Because I thought I could still do it all. Take care of you, run on the track team, be top in my class. And act as if I hadn't just screwed up my entire life in one night in the back of Roger Bass's Chevy LeMans."

"*Everyone* has a night in the back of a LeMans, Penny. You can't blame yourself for that."

"I lost control. I stepped away from the plan." I shook my head, not wanting to remember those days when I'd abandoned responsibilities for a guy with a leather jacket and a nice car. "It was God's way of punishing me."

"It was not! You can't think that."

But I did and had for years. I'd always believed it was some karmic revenge for my cockiness, my rash decision to lose my virginity. To break away from all that responsibility and pressure.

"Georgia, I was supposed to be the responsible one, the one in charge, the one you were supposed to be able to rely on."

"You know who was supposed to do all those things, Penny?" Georgia said, dipping her face to meet mine, so that I couldn't run away from the subject. "Who was supposed to warn us about getting in the back of a LeMans? Who was supposed to tell us to use birth control and wear clean underwear and never wipe snot on our sleeves? Our mother. And she didn't. She left you to raise me, and whatever mistakes you think you made, were nothing. Look at me, I turned out okay. As far as I'm concerned, you did the best damned job you could. Do *not* blame yourself for what happened."

I made a very unladylike sound. "I got pregnant and I lost the baby. I never even carried it to term. How can I not blame myself?" I turned away. "I couldn't even do that right. I had to keep on going, pretending everything was okay, that losing a baby at five months was no big deal."

"You were sixteen, Penny. You were allowed to make mistakes."

I shook my head, and when I did, I realized tears had been streaming down my face. They'd been there all these years, but I'd ignored them, just as I'd ignored everything in my life, my marriage, that had started slipping out of my control. "No, I wasn't. I had you. I had—"

"Don't you dare say responsibilities," Georgia cut

in. "Because you also had a responsibility to live your own life. You have never done that, Pen. You have worked to take care of everyone else—me, Mom, Dave. To keep this house perfect, your job perfect, your life perfect. And at what price?"

"If I keep it under control, no one gets hurt." But even as the words I'd told myself nearly my entire life left my mouth, I knew I was lying. I had done my damnedest to control every aspect of my days, from the neat paths I vacuumed into the living room carpet to the way I folded T-shirts, to the rigid hours I kept at work. And in the end, it turned out nothing had been perfect except for the freakin' carpet.

Georgia came around me, her big blue eyes soft with concern. "Did you ever tell Dave about the baby?"

I shook my head.

"Maybe," Georgia began, laying a soft hand on my arm. "Maybe if you'd opened up to him…" She didn't finish the sentence, didn't blame me.

But I sure did.

"Dave wanted kids," I told her, realizing now where the road had diverged. I'd made wrong choices, and so had Dave. If I'd told him then…where would we be now? Divorced? A happy little family? Or something in between? "He wanted them with me and when I didn't agree, he went to Susan. But she had her own reasons for saying no. And then, he found Annie, who had more than enough kids to go around. Is that where I failed him?"

"No," Georgia said, placing a hand on mine. "That's where *he* failed *you*. If kids was a deal breaker, then he should have had the balls, pardon my French, to divorce you instead of doing what he did."

"Yeah, he should have," I agreed as we took our seats. On that point, I had no argument. It would have hurt, but a divorce five years ago would have had a lot less human fallout than what Dave had done. "I should have spoken up more. Questioned him. Seen the signs instead of being blind." I drew in a breath, let it go, feeling lighter than I had in years. "Either way, I know the truth now and, hey," I said, forcing a tone of lightness into a situation that had been gloomy for far too long, "Harvey and I got a trophy out of it."

Georgia leaned back against the sofa, surprise in her features. "Wow. You really have changed."

"Not too much." I reached into my back pocket and pulled out the list I'd made days ago in the hotel. Like all my lists, it had neat little check marks beside accomplished tasks, and a few more added rows for new tasks.

Georgia laughed. "Now I know you're my sister and not some pod twin."

"There is one more thing," I said. "And if you could stay while I look at it, I'd appreciate it."

"Sis, I'm here for the duration. I brought my toothbrush, my pj's and a jug of wine. I figured *I'd* take care of *you* for once."

The tears rose to my eyes again, but this time from gratitude and love. "I could use some of that." I leaned forward and gave Georgia a quick hug. "You're the best."

She hugged me back, her embrace strong and secure, holding me up as much as I had held her up over the years. Odd, really, how this whole bizarre set of circumstances had brought me closer to my sister. It had done something nothing else in our lives had ever accomplished—equalized us. It wasn't that Georgia had grown up or I had gotten younger. We'd simply found common ground in supporting each other.

I rose, crossed to my bag and retrieved the box Annie had given me. I'd tried a dozen times on the way home to go through it alone, but every time, I'd hesitated, not quite sure I wanted to see what was in there.

"A box? How mysterious," Georgia said when I laid it on the sofa between us.

I took a deep breath, then turned the latch of the heavy fireproof box and opened the lid. At the top was a letter, in an envelope marked "Penny," in Dave's tight handwriting.

I gasped. Clearly, he had known that, someday, I would find out. And he had done the one thing I'd never thought Dave was capable of doing.

Prepared for the future.

For now, I put the letter aside unread, then dug farther into the box. There were some insurance papers for Harvey. "He insured the dog," I said, laughing. "Now *that* I expect out of Dave."

"What else?"

"Not much," I said, shuffling through an old collar of Harvey's, a contract signed years ago with Matt, some business cards for a lawyer and a vet, the former I figured would lead to the will, the latter would give me a distemper shot if I needed it after the will was read.

"There's a set of keys," I said, picking them up and holding them to the light. I didn't recognize them. "House keys, but not to this house."

"Oh," Georgia said. "*Oh*."

Dread sank inside me. "Do you think it means there's another one?" My heart leaped into my throat.

I couldn't do this again. I couldn't find numbers four and five and go on indefinitely through an entire country of Mrs. Reynoldses.

"It could mean something else," Georgia said. But her face scrunched up in doubt.

"Like what? That he has a vacation home in Hawaii? A condo in Canada?"

She shrugged one shoulder. "Maybe."

"Or that he has a whole other life with another family, somewhere else in the country?"

"Dave had a lot of energy, Pen, but I don't think he had enough to keep *four* wives happy."

I clutched the keys in my hand and felt the hard metal dig into my palm. After all I had been through, I was a changed person but not a glutton for punishment. I had no desire to make another road trip to hear another woman sing Dave's praises. "I hope you're right."

"Read the letter," she said, nudging it toward me. "Maybe that'll help."

Dear Penny,
If you've made it to Annie's, then you know it all. I'm sorry, Penny. I never meant to hurt you.

When I married you, I thought… Well, I thought we'd become Dick and Jane. You did, I didn't. I always felt like I was playing a really long game of charades.

I started with the dog, and never intended to go any further than that. Then Harvey's career took off, and before I knew it, I was living a lie that dwarfed them all. I couldn't share it with you, so I looked for someone I could tell.

Vinny once told me the key to working with a dog is communication, both the spoken and the unspoken kind. I should have talked more, said more, and most of all, told you before all this got out of hand.

Please live your life, Penny. Don't retreat to your office and those damned numbers. Love someone, Pen. And if he asks you about bringing home a dog or a cat, or hell, a bald eagle, think about it.

In case you doubted it, you were always the first for me. The woman who captured my heart from the very beginning. You were all I dreamed of—and more than I could deserve.

Love,

Dave

"Well," Georgia said when I was done, "do you think that says he has a fourth wife waiting in the wings?"

"No." I clutched the letter to my chest, taking comfort in his words, in the message from the Dave I used to know.

And love.

I couldn't hate him, as much as I wanted to. I didn't love him as I had before all of this—the betrayals had colored my feelings forever—but I understood him a little better.

The phone rang, and I rose to answer it, leaving the letter on the sofa. "Hello?"

"Penny!" Lillian, my mother-in-law, nearly shouted into the phone. "I've been trying to reach you for days. Aren't you answering your cell phone anymore?"

"I'm sorry, Lillian. I just got home and I must have forgotten all about my phone. I turned it off when I was away." I had never told Lillian where I went and wasn't about to just drop it out there. "And then I never remembered to turn it back on." If there was ever a sign that I had changed, that was it.

"That isn't like you at all."

I laughed. "I know."

"I hate to ask this, because I know you've just gotten home but…" Lillian paused. "I need to see you."

"Now? I was planning on coming down for Christmas, Lillian."

"It can't wait that long. I'm…" She paused again. "I'm really worried about Dave's estate."

"If it's money you need—"

"No, I don't need money." On the other end, she let out a nervous gust. I had never heard prim, perfect Lillian stressed or overwrought, not even during the funeral. She'd cried, yes, but throughout it all, she'd still been her proper self. "There's something I need to ask you about. Something…extra that Dave had."

"You know about Susan?"

"Who's Susan?"

The confusion in Lillian's voice was real. She hadn't known about the other wives, which in a weird way, made me feel better, because it meant I hadn't been the only woman in Dave's life left out of the secret.

Nevertheless, this wasn't the kind of information to tell Lillian over the phone. I needed time to break it to her gently, hopefully with nothing fragile nearby. She'd loved Dave, with a fierceness that bordered on overprotective. Telling her that her son had wives scattered around the country wasn't going to go well.

I promised Lillian I'd leave on the first flight tomorrow, then said goodbye and returned to the living room. "Well, Harvey," I said, "looks like our journey's not over yet. You ready for another road trip?"

Harvey sprang to life, dancing on the sofa and pirouetting on my cushions.

I took that as a yes.

CHAPTER 23

Two weeks to the day after my husband died, I got off a plane at the Orlando International Airport, rented a car and drove to my mother-in-law's house, Harvey at my side. He pranced around the interior of the rental car, clearly glad to be out of the Port-a-Puppy bag I'd used on the plane.

Every few miles, I stopped and let him out on the grassy roadside. The rental car, after all, wasn't lined with plastic and I wasn't taking any chances.

I pulled up to Lillian's house, a small town house in a retirement community that sported a golf course, swimming pool and community center where regular bingo nights were held.

The place also came with several good catches, Lillian had once said, if a lady didn't mind dating a guy over the age of seventy-five who might or might not have all his own teeth.

It had been eight years since I'd been to Lillian's

house. Dave and I had been meaning to come down here and visit her, but I was always busy with tax season and by the time April 15 passed, the urge to flee the Massachusetts cold had passed. She came up every Christmas, and Dave had gone to her house quite often over the years, but I'd never seemed to find a good time to make the trip.

With the warm Florida sunshine on my face and shoulders, plus a forty-degree leap in temperature from the state I'd just left, I couldn't imagine now what could have been more important, or more relaxing, than this.

Lillian answered the door on the first knock. Her eyes widened in joy, and at first, I thought she was looking at me, then noticed her focus had dropped about a foot lower, the smile on her face not for me, but for—

Harvey.

"Oh, Harvey! You're here! And you're safe!" She reached forward, taking the dog out of my arms, holding him close to her chest, nearly smothering him with affection. "I was so worried about you, baby."

I stared at my mother-in-law, coddling and cooing to my husband's secret, money-making dog. "You knew about Harvey?"

Remorse shaded Lillian's light green eyes. She nodded. "Dave made me promise not to tell you.

Then, after he passed away, there didn't seem to be an easy way to mention it. I thought if you came down here, I could break the news of the dog gently, and together we could figure out where Harvey was."

"Susan brought him to me after the funeral. I've had him ever since." A wry smile crossed my lips. "I couldn't find an easy way to tell you because I didn't know you knew."

It all seemed like a badly written Abbott and Costello script.

Lillian's perfectly penciled brows knit together in confusion. "You keep mentioning a Susan. Did she work with Dave?"

I didn't want to stand here on Lillian's azalea-filled porch and tell her that her son was a bigamist. I didn't want to ever tell her but knew someday it would come out and I didn't want Lillian to be as sideswiped by the information as I had been. "There were some things I couldn't tell you over the phone, either. Let's go inside and talk."

She nodded, as if she'd anticipated I'd be coming down here with more than a plane ticket. "I have something to show you first, Penny." She waved me inside, then lowered Harvey to the floor.

As I walked into Lillian's neat, contemporary town

house, past the living room and down the hall that led
to the two bedrooms, I prayed I wasn't about to pull
open door number one and see a shrine set up to Dave's
wives. Or some secret love nest behind door number
two that Dave had created for in-between dog gigs.

When Lillian opened the door on the right and
stepped back, Harvey bounded straight into the room.
My gaze swept over the space, but it took a good five
seconds to register that what I was seeing wasn't a
shrine to Dave or his bigamy—

But to Harvey.

The dog's name curved in huge blue block letters
across the far wall, arching over a white silk-covered
doggie bed loaded with colorful pillows, all sporting
cartoon drawings of Jack Russell terriers at play. A
massive wicker basket overflowing with dog toys sat
in one corner, in the other, a mini-reclining chair,
decked out in navy dog-resistant fabric and embroidered with Harvey's name on the headrest.

Shelves held more toys and what appeared to be a
lifetime supply of rawhide bones and Beggin' Strips.
A pair of ceramic food and water bowls sat on a bone-
shaped plastic mat, again decorated with Harvey's
name and a smattering of brightly colored paw prints.

The closet door was ajar, revealing a puppy-size

wardrobe twice the size of my own. Inside, every costume imaginable, from cowboy to clown, hung off satin hangers. Matching hats filled the top shelf, the pile so big they'd started to teeter over the edge.

"This is all Harvey's?"

Lillian nodded. "A lot of it was gifts from admiring fans. Harvey's not a diva, or whatever it is that a male star is called. He's never even been a real picky dog. Some pet company sent that bed to Dave for Harvey, hoping they could get a photo of him on it, but Harvey—" she laughed a little "—that dog had a mind of his own and he wouldn't sleep on that silly thing for a year."

Harvey darted around the room, sniffing his things, pulling out this toy, then discarding it for that one. He leaped at the shelves, but lacked about four feet of height to reach the prized Beggin' Strips.

"But how… Why…" I couldn't even voice the questions tumbling around in my head. Shock and hurt that Lillian too had been involved—and helped keep this secret from me—rendered me nearly mute.

"Let's leave Harvey to his things and go on out to the lanai." She gave my hand a gentle pat. "I know you have questions. It's high time I answered them."

I followed my mother-in-law out to the sunroom,

waiting while she returned to the kitchen to grab a jug of iced tea out of the refrigerator and a pair of tall thin glasses from the cabinet. She filled them with ice, then put the whole ensemble on a porcelain tray, adding sugar and long, skinny spoons.

So like Lillian—in the midst of major upheaval, she was still a damned good hostess.

We sat in opposite wicker chairs, the Florida sun warming the yellow-and-blue room and giving it a bright, happy feel. I waited, sipping at my tea, knowing Lillian would tell me what she had to say in her own time.

And also delaying the inevitable of telling her what I knew.

"How much do you know?" she asked.

"Everything but this," I said, then remembered the keys in my pocket. "I think."

CHAPTER 24

"You know about Matt and Vinny and the tour?" Lillian said, clearly not the only surprised one in the room.

I nodded. "I just came from the Dog-Gone-Good Show. Harvey won Best Dog Overall, as well as the talent portion."

A smile stole across Lillian's normally still features. "That's good. Dave would have liked that."

"You were the one who kept Harvey between shows?" It all made sense now. Neither Susan nor Annie had housed Harvey. I'd just assumed he stayed with either Matt or Vinny or at some fancy-dancy dog boarding house when he wasn't with Dave. I hadn't even considered that Lillian was involved.

"Dave came to me, after you said no to the idea of a dog." She shook a sugar packet, the granules settling into the base, before she tore off the top. "I'm not blaming you, Penny. If Harvey had been a cat or a cockatoo, I would have said no, too. I've just always loved dogs, especially Jack Russells because I had one when I was a little girl. For me, deciding to take in Harvey was easy." She stirred some sugar into her glass. Ice cubes clinked together, a quiet melody underlying Lillian's words. "After Dave's father died, I was lonely. Really lonely. Harvey, bless his little heart, helped fill that gap. He gave me something to do, something to look forward to every day."

The chronology fell into place. Dave had found the dog, about a month after his father passed away, and at the same time as I'd been promoted, thus making me busier and less available if Dave had needed to talk. And much less open to the idea of a pet.

"I should have been there for Dave," I said, understanding now, after going through the shock of losing someone, how much the death of his father must have hurt, and how little I had listened in those days, thinking he was just fine. He was a guy; he didn't break down and cry. He went to work, more than ever before. I'd thought by making sure he had everything packed, by printing out his itinerary and by keeping everything smoothly running in the house, I was doing what helped Dave. I'd been so busy doing "the right thing," that I'd never even noticed the chasm opening up between us. "He needed me, but I didn't even see it. He never broke down, never had an off day."

"Oh, you know Dave, sweetie. That man would have had a smile on his face if he was sinking on the *Titanic*." She patted my knee. "He wasn't much for sharing his feelings, even when he was little. If he needed you, he should have spoken up."

"I was his wife. I should have known."

"Bullshit," Lillian said, surprising me with the curse out of her perfectly made-up mouth. "Whoever said that is an idiot. I was married for forty years to Larry Reynolds and I didn't know much more than the way he took his steak. Most men are impossible to read. They keep everything inside, like they're saving it for a rainy day."

I smoothed the condensation off my glass and then inhaled a deep breath. I had to tell her sometime. "Lillian, it was more than that. Dave married someone else."

She paled and grew very still. "Married someone else? When? Before you?"

"Five years ago. While he was still married to me. That's who Susan is. His other wife."

Lillian's mouth formed a perfect, open O. The facts came together in her mind, as they had in mine, and

I saw her fit missing pieces into her own mental puzzle. "That explains a lot."

"I've met Susan and you would like her. You also would have liked Annie, who was Dave's…friend, I guess. He never married her." I left off the rest of the details with the Annie story. Lillian didn't need to know it all. I thought again of the keys and where they fit into this picture.

"My son was juggling three women? This from the kid who couldn't keep up with the track team at practice?"

I laughed, more heartily than I had in weeks. "I guess so. If it helps, though, I think he did it for more or less unselfish reasons."

Lillian sighed and put her glass down. She watched a blue jay flutter against a feeder hanging off a wrought-iron shepherd's hook in the yard, spilling as much seed as it ate. "When Dave was young, I was so busy, wrapped up in helping Larry get his law practice off the ground, then Kevin came along and he was so colicky…" She ran a hand over her face. "Dave and his father, they just didn't get along, oil and water, those two. Their personalities clashed from the first bottle Larry tried to give to Dave." She shook her head, eyes filled with bittersweet memories. "Dave had his issues, too, Penny," she went on. "He tried to get close to his dad, Lord knows he did, by helping him wherever he could, but for some reason, it never worked. Larry was a hard man to live with, God rest his soul, and I think Dave might have grown up needing that reassurance that he was loved. I'm not exactly a warm and fuzzy mother. I was always good at the baking-cookies and holding-birthday-parties part, but the cuddling over a story, that was never my strong suit. There always seemed to be another dish to wash or someone asking me to find a lost glove. Dave, I think, got kind of lost in the shuffle." Lillian leaned forward and touched my knee. "You were good for him in many ways because you kept him on track, made him accountable. You know Dave. He'd run off on a tangent here or there, and forget to pay his bills or register the car."

"But I didn't give him what he needed emotionally."

"And I bet he didn't tell you what he needed either, did he?"

I shook my head.

Lillian's gaze grew misty and she turned away, staring at a misshapen ceramic ashtray Dave had made in art class when he'd been a little boy. "Dave talked to me all the time about how much he wanted children."

"I didn't give him that, either." I swallowed back the ache in my throat.

"Dave may have been a great father, but he wanted kids for all the wrong reasons. I think he thought they'd fill up the holes inside him." She stirred her drink again but didn't sip it. "I told him, over and over, that a child required love to be *given*, that they weren't there to feed *you* the love. I don't think he ever understood that."

"Maybe that's why Dave kept looking for a woman who could do everything. Give him children, love his dog and be able to read his thoughts."

"Instead of realizing no one person can be everything to another." Lillian smiled. "I loved my son and I always will, but he wasn't perfect."

I watched the bright blue bird return to the feeder, dart in and grab a sunflower seed. "Neither was I."

"You didn't go find another husband, though."

"Yeah, there is that." I drank some tea, then put the glass down. Lillian immediately refilled it, the action coming so quick I knew it was more instinct than intrusion. "But I'm okay with the wife thing now. It doesn't mean I won't go home and throw darts at his picture someday."

Lillian laughed. "I may be his mother but I'm also

a woman, too, and I wouldn't blame you one bit if you did that."

Then I told Lillian what Susan had told me, how Dave had helped her. I did the same with Annie's story. I filtered it through the protective lens of a daughter-in-law who truly did like her mother-in-law and didn't want to see Lillian any more hurt than she already was by the loss of her eldest child.

We laughed, we cried, and we mourned the man both of us had loved, in very different ways. At the end, I handed over the keys I'd found in Dave's box, knowing now that they were to Lillian's house. She thanked me, then stared at the keys for a long moment, finally seeing in the glint of metal, I thought, that her son was gone.

Then Lillian steeled herself, leaned over and hugged me tight. "I want you to take Harvey home with you."

"But, Lillian, he's been yours for years."

"He's already closer to you." We looked down at the floor and noticed Harvey, at my feet, with a pile of toys he had dragged into the sunroom while we were talking. He'd mounded them beside my shoes, as if giving me a mountain of vinyl squeaky gifts. "And besides, I think that right now, the two of you need each other. To heal. He'll give you something to do,

Penny, in the days ahead. A reason to get up in the morning. Because there are going to be days when this will hit you as hard as a brick wall and you're going to need a reason to move forward."

"What are you going to do?"

She smiled and looked out over the grassy space behind the sunroom. "I've been thinking about getting one of those Chihuahuas. Spoil the heck out of her, dressing her up in raincoats and tutus. I'm an old lady, I'm expected to have a dog like that. And, it'll be fun to see if I can teach an old dog new tricks."

"You mean a young dog."

"No," Lillian said, laughing. "I meant *this* old dog. Change is good and it's about time I had one."

I left my mother-in-law later that afternoon, promising to return again in a few months so that she and Harvey could see each other. Walking away from Lillian's house seemed to close one more chapter. There might always be, I realized, a few loose threads in Dave's life. You couldn't tear apart the fabric of a life and not leave a few things unconnected. But I had enough of them tied together that I could stop searching and start concentrating on me.

"If this Chihuahua works out," I whispered to Harvey as we left, "you better practice your bullfighting. I have a feeling you won't be the only dog in the retirement community going after her heart."

Harvey let out a bark that said he was up to the challenge.

CHAPTER 25

I sat in the living room of the house I'd once shared with my husband, staring at his picture on the mantel, sipping a glass of wine. A fire roared in the fireplace, that day's newspaper lay in a disarrayed pile on the floor, spun out of control by Harvey's frantic feet. Half of me wanted to stack the papers again, to lay them on the coffee table in a pristine pile in alphabetical section order, but I had learned that life was too short to be stacking the newspaper and vacuuming straight lines into my carpet.

I was alone, except for Harvey, and had been for several weeks. At first, it had been harder than I expected to be alone. My husband had traveled all the time, I'd thought I was used to solitary life. But with the knowledge that he wasn't going to walk through the door, that he wasn't going to be the one to plant the mums, I had to find a new existence. So I planted my own mums, hired a neighborhood kid to mow the lawn and repainted my bedroom yellow.

I'd spent a lot of time going over the past in those first couple weeks, before I finally realized I couldn't change it so there wasn't much sense in rehashing it.

On the notepad on my lap—I may have changed, but I hadn't gotten rid of my lists—I scribbled the words "Life List." I wrote a numeral one and then added a single item: Move forward.

That was enough for now.

When I was done, I raised my glass toward my husband's picture, still sitting on the mantel and, thus far, unmarred by darts. "Thank you, Dave, for sending me on a journey that changed my life."

He smiled back at me, the same perpetual smile that Olan Mills had captured a few years back.

"And thank you for the dog. About him, you were right. The other wives, not such a good idea."

Dave kept on smiling.

I would love him, maybe for the rest of my life, but I doubted I would ever truly understand what had driven my husband to keep all these secrets from me instead of simply having a conversation and trying to mend the broken toy he already had, as Annie had said.

Now it was time to put all this behind me. I glanced again at the list.

Move forward.

I picked up the phone and dialed a number I had memorized from the first time I saw it inside the box. Matt picked up on the first ring. "Hi," I said, not sure yet what I wanted to say. Writing "move forward" was a lot easier than actually doing it.

"Hi," he said back, delighted surprise raising his tone a few notes. "How are you?"

"Much better. Doing okay all by myself, which surprises me. I even fixed the faucet last week."

"Glad to hear it."

"I was thinking," I began, fingering the notebook beside me, the same one that Dave had left with Harvey's things. I ran my nail down the itinerary of the six-city tour. One thing that was good about being a workaholic, I had enough vacation built up to take a month, maybe two, off from work. "I'd like to take a trip. To Denver, Salt Lake City, San Francisco, San Diego. Maybe a couple other places, too."

I could practically hear Matt grinning as he recognized the list of cities. "Planning on taking a certain dog along?"

"I'll have to. I haven't mastered the picking-out-the-banana trick yet. Harvey's still the king at that."

Matt laughed. "Do you want some company?"

"Yes," I said. "That would be nice."

"Good." The huskiness of that one word sent a remix of the music he'd played in his kiss zipping through my veins. "Then I'll meet you in Denver on the twelfth."

Matt and I talked a little while longer, then we said goodbye and hung up.

Anticipation rose inside me, a feeling I hadn't had in years. Would something come of the relationship between me and Matt? It was still too soon to tell and too soon for me to want anyone else in my life on anything other than a part-time basis. Two months after losing my husband, I was still working through being alone.

I'd divided the estate evenly between the four of us, because I'd figured that was what Dave would have wanted—for Susan, Annie and his mother to be taken care of as well as me. There was plenty to divide. Matt had been right—Harvey was a cash cow. There'd been enough for Susan to finish her education, for Annie to buy a house and pay off the medical bills. I'd even sent a little to Norm and Rita, and their new baby boy, who they had named Harvey. Poor kid. His photo sat to the left of Dave's on the mantel. Norm had traded his singing ambitions for a job as a mechanic, but with the check I planned on sending them for their wedding gift, I hoped Norm would have enough money to afford a few days off for the upcoming *American Idol* tryouts. Who knew? Maybe I'd have two performers in my life.

Vinny still suffered the occasional flashback, but had told me he was planning on taking a Pekingese onstage next week. I asked him about the dog treats and he'd rattled something over the phone. "Plastic, baby, that's the solution. Put the dog treats in this thing and it protects my banana, if you know what I mean."

I'd had a letter from Susan last week, telling me about her budding relationship with Jerry, another from Annie today, saying that Max was on his way to being a star, if she could just get him to stop eating the Legos.

Someday, I'd stop by and see them again, but for now, I was working on the "Just Penny" campaign.

If you asked me, it was going quite well.

"Harvey," I said, to the dog who was never far from my side and who had, as Lillian had promised, given me a reason to get up on the days when I'd rather have stayed in bed. "You up to another road trip?"

The dog did his frantic circle dance, spinning the newspaper across the room, then dashed away, returning a moment later with a clump of silver and gold in his mouth.

"My keys," I said, laughing. "Are you a little anxious to go?"

He barked, then turned around and disappeared again. When he came back with a box of plastic wrap in his mouth, I knew Harvey was ready to move forward.

And so was I.